Carter flexed his stiff fingers.

"Hold on tight, you guys," he said. "Here I come."

"We've got you!" Buzz said. All three of the others gripped the pole around the base, watching as Carter let himself off the tiny shelf where he'd been waiting.

Gripping the ledge with both hands, he lowered himself toward the top of the bamboo. One foot hooked the pole, and then both legs wrapped around it as he came low enough.

The idea was to let go of the ledge, one hand at a time, then press his palms into the cliff wall and use leverage, leg strength, and gravity to lower himself the next few crucial feet.

But the moment Carter let go with his first hand, he could tell it wasn't going to work. His other hand slipped off too soon, and he slid faster and farther than he'd intended, several feet down the pole. He'd barely taken hold of the bamboo before his own weight forced it to pull away from the wall.

"Wait!" Jane screamed, but there was nothing Carter could do. The pole came unstoppably into a vertical position, and then kept on going. The next thing he knew, it was falling toward the rocks.

"JUMP!" Buzz yelled.

The **STRANDED** Series

Book 1: **STRANDED**

Book 2: **TRIAL BY FIRE**

Book 3: **SURVIVORS**

JEFF PROBST

and CHRIS TEBBETTS

SCHOLASTIC INC.

ISBN 978-0-545-73474-5

12 11 10 9 8 7 6 5 4 3 2 1   14 15 16 17 18 19/0

Printed in the U.S.A.   40

First Scholastic printing, March 2014

After the first *Stranded* was published in February 2013, I began to hear from lots of young readers eager to share their thoughts about *Stranded* and the characters and, most importantly, what they thought should happen next!

Some of you reached out in person and others reached me through @jeffprobst on Twitter. I loved hearing from all of you, and your ideas were very helpful.

I want to personally thank a few of you who read this third book when it was still in the manuscript stage: Sophia, Julia, Keegan, Leo, and Ireland. You are true collaborators on this book. You should take a copy to your teachers and ask for extra credit. (Sophia and Julia, your note about the jellyfish saved the day!)

I hope you all enjoy the next part of the *Stranded* adventure, and remember . . .

"The adventure you're ready for is the one you get!"

—*JP*

Several people who helped us get our story off the ground for *Stranded Book 1* were kind enough to offer some additional help along the way. Thank you (again!) to our sailing expert Jill Kuramoto; teachers Angela Galyean and Paul Lasher, along with their wonderful students at Hinesburg Community School; the man behind the big bang, Kyle Jablonski; writing and critique partners Jan Donley, Barbara Gregorich, Vicki Hayes, Ruth Horowitz, and Joe Nusbaum; and all-around muse Jonathan Radigan.

A few indispensable newbies deserve our gratitude as well. Many thanks to Dave Bernheisel from the Lightship Overfalls in Lewes, Delaware, for his nautical insights; to Dr. Ramona Salins, who detailed the hazards of wound infection for us; and to Simon Ross and Ian Tucker from the *Survivor* pyro team for a couple of truly bright ideas.

Lastly, one more enormous thank-you to our editor at Puffin, Jen Bonnell, whose voice, insight, and patience were an integral part of this storytelling adventure.

—*CT*

CHAPTER 1

Buzz Diaz looked over the edge. Straight down from where he stood, at the bottom of a hundred-foot cliff, ocean waves lapped at the rocky shoreline of Nowhere Island.

"We're going to have to climb down," Carter said.

"Tell me you're joking!" Buzz shouted. The gusting wind forced them to yell even though they were standing close together.

"I'm not joking."

"But this could kill us."

"So could staying up here," Jane chimed in.

"Yeah," Carter agreed, "just a lot more slowly."

Buzz could barely believe they were even having this conversation. The face of the wall they would have to descend was a straight drop. There were only a few places to stand and even fewer to hold on to. One slip and it was over. Nobody could survive that kind of a fall.

Ten minutes ago, they'd been *this close* to getting rescued. He, Carter, and Jane had screamed and waved like crazy as the plane passed over their little island. Buzz's own screams echoed in his head now—STOP! STOP! HELP! PLEASE!—but none of it had done them any good.

The plane was gone. So was the tree bridge they'd crossed to get up here in the first place. It had fallen straight down into the ravine on the opposite side of Lookout Point, and had nearly taken Buzz with it. He was lucky to be alive.

But Buzz wasn't feeling so lucky right now. His stomach swooped every time he looked down the cliff face, or out toward the endless Pacific Ocean that stretched away from the island. It was like looking at infinity from here.

"Are we sure this is the *better* way down?" he asked.

It wasn't a real question. They'd been back and forth across Lookout Point a dozen times. As scary as it would be scaling the ocean-facing cliffs, every other option was even worse. At least on this side, the rock was stepped in a series of plateaus and ledges, as far down as Buzz could see.

"I say we go for it," Carter announced. He nodded to Jane, the youngest of the group. "You ready?" he asked.

"I'm ready," she replied.

Easy for them to say, Buzz thought. Carter was a total jock, and Jane had already proven herself to be a natural climber here on the island.

Not Buzz. He was a natural couch potato, as much as anything else. But none of that meant anything for him anymore. The only real question now was whether he'd rather die from falling a hundred feet or from starving to death on this barren tower of rock.

"Yeah, okay," he said, barely believing the words as they came out of his own mouth. "Let's get this over with."

Carter could see how scared Jane and Buzz were. He was scared, too. Out of his mind. But so what? It didn't change what they had to do.

"I'll go first," he said, and sat himself on the edge of the cliff.

He got no argument from the other two. Carter was the strongest. That was just a fact. If a week on Nowhere Island had taught them nothing else, it was how to face up to hard, cold facts.

It seemed like forever ago that their boat had crashed onto the shore, stranding them here. The storm responsible had also separated them from Uncle Dexter and his first mate on the *Lucky Star*, Joe Kahali. Whether those two were still out there in the South Pacific somewhere was impossible to know. Carter had been the last to see them, just before the waves and high winds tore their life raft away from the *Lucky Star* and they'd disappeared into the night.

Ever since that moment, it had been up to the kids to figure everything out for themselves.

How to make fire and shelter.

How to find food and water.

How to survive.

Carter looked down the cliff face. The next nearest ledge was maybe seven feet below him—a few feet more than his own body length. He and Buzz were the same age, eleven, but Carter was taller. For Buzz, and especially Jane, who was tiny for a nine-year-old, the drop would feel even farther.

As he started to inch himself off the edge, Jane stepped forward and grabbed onto the ragged T-shirt Carter had been wearing for the last week.

"Be careful," she said.

"I'm always careful," Carter said, and grinned at his little sister. It was funny, only because they both knew it wasn't true. Nowhere Island was not a place where you could survive by being careful. You had to take some chances.

Before he could lose his nerve, Carter turned around and eased himself the rest of the way over the lip of the cliff. Pulse racing, and wind whipping in his ears, he lowered his body until he was hanging with arms fully extended. The outcropping he wanted to reach was still a foot or more down. It wasn't far, but if he missed, it was going to be a long drop to the bottom.

This was the moment of truth. He checked the distance to the ledge under his feet one more time. Took a breath. And let go.

Gravity took care of the rest. His palms scraped over the cliff wall, and the gash on his right hand from the day before lit up with a hot flash of pain. Still, it was nothing compared to the rush of the quick drop. With a jolt, he landed on the narrow piece of rock. His whole body shuddered as he found his balance, and he pressed himself into the wall as close as he could get.

Carter didn't even try to catch his breath. That would have to come later. A quick glance down past his heels showed him the vertical maze of ledges and handholds that still waited between this spot and the ground.

Seven feet down. Ninety-something to go.

＊＊＊

Jane followed Carter's example. She turned around

on the rim of the cliff and lowered herself toward the first ledge.

"You can do it, Jane," Buzz said.

Hanging with her face toward the rock, it was a blind descent. When she let go, everything blurred, but Carter was right there as she landed. He put a firm hand on her arm and held tight.

"I've got you," he said. "That wasn't so bad, right?"

Jane only nodded. It was hard to speak with her heart running so fast. It felt as if the wind could scoop in and pull her right off the ledge without warning. Carter was trying to be encouraging, but her brother's wide eyes said otherwise. This was going to be anything *but* easy.

As Buzz started down, Jane and Carter pushed together to make room for him. Buzz moved more cautiously and not nearly as gracefully, but when his feet finally touched down next to them, he let out a huge sigh of relief.

"Okay," he muttered, maybe just to convince himself. "Okay, okay . . . let's keep going."

Level by level, they made their way down the wall,

descending like a human inchworm. Carter would advance first, then Jane, then Buzz, before Carter moved on again. Twice, they had to shuffle sideways along a ledge before they could make the next drop. Their progress was slow but steady.

And then it came to a stop. Carter had just reached a shallow ridge below Jane and Buzz when he held up a hand.

"Don't come down yet," he said.

"Why?" Buzz asked. "What is it?"

They were well past the halfway point. It looked to Jane as if the rocks of the shoreline were no more than thirty feet farther down. But the only thing she could see between where Carter stood and the ground itself was sheer cliff wall. No ledges. No handholds. Nothing.

"Carter? Are we stuck?" Jane asked, trying to stay calm.

"I don't know," Carter said. He craned his neck, looking down, left, and right. "We might be."

"Might be?" Buzz called out, the tension rising in his voice.

Carter didn't respond, but the answer was obvious to Jane. They'd just reached a dead end—fingers clinging to the cliff wall, feet balanced on narrow pieces of rock, and too high up to even think about jumping.

They weren't going anywhere.

CHAPTER 2

Vanessa picked her way along the shoreline, headed for camp as fast as she could go. It was rough, slow hiking over the black sandpapery boulders that rimmed this part of the island. More than once, she slipped and scraped her hands. The tide was coming in, too, and the breaking waves sprayed her with salt water that stung her eyes.

There was good reason to be careful. Any cut or scrape could get infected, and then good luck dealing with that. There was no first-aid kit on the island. No adults. No hospital for a thousand miles. Just *not* getting hurt was like an added responsibility.

Still, it was hard not to rush. There was so much she had to tell the others!

She'd run away from camp before dawn, feeling as if she'd never be able to face Carter, Jane, and Buzz again. Not after what had happened the night before. As the oldest, she was supposed to be looking out for her younger siblings. Instead, she'd fallen asleep on her own watch. Jane's precious journal had dropped into the fire, and then—even worse—the flames had spread to their little bamboo shelter on the beach. Within minutes, the whole thing had burned to the ground.

But all of that was secondary now, compared to what had happened since. Traveling up the shore that morning, Vanessa had stumbled upon a cove none of them knew about. There was a freshwater stream, and an old shipwreck tucked into the inlet. The water alone was like gold in a place like this—plus who knew what other kind of supplies might be waiting for them on that ship?

It was a question she would have answered for herself, if not for the other discovery she'd made. In a clearing overlooking the cove, Vanessa had also found something like a small graveyard. A wooden cross was stuck into the ground there, and a single human skeleton lay in the underbrush.

The remains had most definitely been human. There was no mistaking the shape of the skull she'd seen, or the long arm and leg bones. Vanessa shuddered just thinking about it. Whoever had crashed on the island before them had also died here.

Whether or not she'd mention the graveyard, she wasn't sure yet. It was probably better to focus on the positive news first, she thought. It wouldn't do any good to—

"VANESSA!"

A shout came from somewhere nearby. Right away, Vanessa recognized Buzz's voice, but she couldn't tell where it was coming from. Straight ahead, she could see their familiar beach, where the rocky part of the shoreline gave way to soft sand. She could even see their camp and the burned remains of their shelter. But no Buzz, or anyone else.

"Buzz?" she called out.

"Up here!" he said. "Help!"

Vanessa's gaze traveled up the rock wall on her right—and there, maybe thirty feet off the ground, were Buzz, Jane, and Carter.

Her voice came out in a scream. "What are you doing? How did you get up there?"

"We didn't," Jane said. "We got down."

"What?"

"Just help us!" Carter yelled.

Even from this distance, the fear on their faces was clear. Buzz and Jane both stood balanced on a tiny outcropping that was barely wider than their feet. Carter sat just below them, on his own lip of rock.

Vanessa stepped from black boulder to black boulder, hurrying closer. "Do we still have any rope?" she called up. She hadn't taken any stock of their supplies since the fire.

"Yeah," Carter said, "but that doesn't do us any good. We don't have any way to anchor it up here."

"Can you see some other way for us to climb down?" Buzz called.

Vanessa scanned the cliff face for any kind of

handholds they might reach. "I don't see anything," she said. Behind her, the ocean was at least fifty feet away. It was too far to jump, in any case. The beach was off to the side, and much closer, but landing in sand wasn't like landing in water. Any of them could easily break a bone—or worse, if they hit the rocks.

"There has to be something," Jane said. "Think!"

Vanessa's mind raced. She squinted over at their beach camp, looking for anything they might use. Mostly, she just saw the burned-out shelter. Several charred pieces of bamboo lay in the sand.

"Anything?" Buzz called down. "There must be a way—"

"Bamboo!" Vanessa shouted as it came to her.

"What?" Jane shouted.

There was no time to waste. "I'll be right back!" Vanessa said, already rushing off the rocks, down to the sand, and into camp.

The axe was right there, next to the dead fire pit. She snatched it up and kept moving. The bamboo grew in a grove just a few minutes up the beach, but she'd still have to find a long enough piece. Even then, could this actually work? Would she be able to get the others off that cliff wall? Or would it end in disaster?

The answer to all of it was—maybe. But now was not the time for questions.

Watching Vanessa run off, Jane wiggled her toes. After standing on the tiny ledge for so long, her foot was starting to fall asleep. The sun beat down on them, and her hands were sweaty where she tried to grip the rock wall behind her.

She couldn't stop thinking about the plane, either. It had flown right over the island, close enough to show the blue markings on its wings and tail. It was like torture, thinking about where they might have been by now if the plane had spotted them. Wrapped up in a blanket with something to eat? On their way back to civilization? On their way home?

"Jane, you okay?" Carter asked from his spot just below her on the wall.

"I will be," she told him, even though it felt like

a lie. It was always harder when she thought about home. But complaining wasn't going to help anyone.

Finally, Vanessa reappeared on the beach. Jane could see her dragging a long green cane of freshly cut bamboo behind her.

"I'm coming!" she shouted. "Just hold on!"

All Jane, Buzz, or Carter could do was watch as Vanessa worked her way back to the rocks of Dead Man's Shelf. That was Jane's name for it—this piece of shoreline where their sailboat had crashed into the island.

When Vanessa got there, she hauled the long pole up onto the rocks and struggled to get it into place. Bit by bit, she managed to pivot the bamboo until one end was directly beneath the spot where Jane waited with her brothers. Vanessa positioned herself at the opposite end of the pole and lifted it up, walking it hand over hand into an upright position.

It was awkward going. Twice, Vanessa lost her grip and had to start over. But on the third try, the bamboo slowly went vertical, and then just past, until it was leaning against the cliff face.

Jane's heart sunk. The bamboo was *almost* tall enough, but not quite. The top of the pole had come to rest a few feet below the ledge where Carter was perched.

"Can you get to it?" Vanessa called up.

"I don't think so!" Jane said.

"Yes," Carter answered over her, his voice set with determination. Already, he was lying flat on his piece of ledge. With one arm extended, he was just able to wrap a hand around the top of the bamboo cane.

"See? We can do this," Carter said. "Come on, Jane. You first."

Jane wasn't so sure, but she edged herself off the rock where she'd been standing with Buzz for the last hour or more. She eased down into the tiny space next to Carter and stood between his legs.

"I can hold the pole steady from up here while you slide down," Carter said. "Then Buzz can go next."

"But then what are you going to do?" Jane asked, alarmed all over again. It wasn't a hundred-foot drop anymore, but it was still enough to kill any of them if they fell.

"We'll figure that out later," Carter said.

"But what if—"

"What if what, Jane?" her brother snapped. "Someone has to go last."

He was right, Jane knew. There was no good answer here, and nothing left to talk about. Heart thudding, she squeezed down to a sitting position next to Carter. He kept one hand on the bamboo. With the other, he hooked Jane under her arm and helped ease her off the ledge until she could reach the pole.

First, Jane's legs wrapped around it. Then as she came low enough, she grabbed on with both hands.

"Have you got it?" Carter asked.

"I . . . guess," Jane said. For some reason, the bamboo had looked thicker and sturdier from above. The whole thing bowed under her weight, bringing her even closer to the cliff wall. But there was no going back now. With a deep breath, she let go just enough to slide down a few feet, and then stopped again.

"Good job, Janie!" Vanessa called out. "Keep going!"

Jane loosened her grip again and dropped a bit farther.

Then again, and again.

The bamboo burned against her skin as she went. It wasn't a smooth ride, but the ground came up quickly. Soon, she was standing safely on the rocks next to Vanessa.

There was no time for talking. The girls quickly positioned themselves on either side of the pole as Buzz got ready to work his way down.

His descent was slower than Jane's had been. His body scraped against the cliff face as he squeaked his way along, foot by foot. By the time he touched down and let go of the bamboo, his arms and legs were marred with painful-looking, deep-red burn marks. Still, he looked more relieved than anything.

Now came the really tricky part. It was Carter's turn.

Carter flexed his stiff fingers. His hands were raw from gripping rock, and the gash on his palm had opened up. This wasn't going to be easy.

"Hold on tight, you guys," he said. "Here I come."

"We've got you!" Buzz said. All three of the others gripped the pole around the base, watching as Carter let himself off the tiny shelf where he'd been waiting.

Gripping the ledge with both hands, he lowered himself toward the top of the bamboo. One foot hooked the pole, and then both legs wrapped around it as he came low enough.

The idea was to let go of the ledge, one hand at a time, then press his palms into the cliff wall and use leverage, leg strength, and gravity to lower himself the next few crucial feet.

But the moment Carter let go with his first hand, he could tell it wasn't going to work. His other hand slipped off too soon, and he slid faster and farther than he'd intended, several feet down the pole. He'd barely taken hold of the bamboo before his own weight forced it to pull away from the wall.

"Wait!" Jane screamed, but there was nothing Carter could do. The pole came unstoppably into a vertical position, and then kept on going. The next thing he knew, it was falling toward the rocks.

"JUMP!" Buzz yelled.

He saw Buzz throw himself against the pole and felt a hard jerk from below. The bamboo's direction shifted. It was falling toward the beach now. In the fraction of a second Carter had left, he realized what Buzz meant for him to do. He thrust as hard as he could, pushing himself away from the falling pole. His eyes took in a blur of rock, sea, and sky—just before he landed in the sand. A shock of pain came up through his legs. He absorbed what he could and rolled several times before coming to a stop.

He was on his back. His eyes were squeezed shut, and he tried to figure out if anything was broken.

"Carter!" Jane's voice came from nearby. The others were there now, kneeling next to him. Someone's hand was on his arm.

"Can you sit up?" Vanessa said.

Carter blinked several times and squinted into the hot sun. He wiggled his toes. Bent his knees.

"I think so," he said.

As they got him onto his feet, it was a relief to find that he could walk on his own. The only real pain came from the throbbing cut on his hand. But that didn't seem like much, compared to what could have happened.

The point was, he'd made it down in one piece.

They all had. And they'd done it together.

CHAPTER 3

Back at camp, everyone flopped out in the shade. It had been a long morning. Vanessa could hardly wait to tell the others about the cove she'd found, but they had a story of their own to tell first.

Jane explained that a plane had flown by that morning. Vanessa had never even heard it from where she'd been.

It was the first and only plane any of them had seen since they'd been stranded here a week ago. Despite Carter, Jane, and Buzz's best efforts, everything had gone horribly wrong. The tree bridge they'd been using to reach Lookout Point was gone now, and they'd never gotten a real chance to signal the plane.

Tears showed in Buzz's eyes as he told his part of the story.

"I'm really sorry, you guys," he said. "If I hadn't fallen off the tree bridge, we could have gotten up there in time. We might have been on our way home by now—"

He stopped and bit his lip. That word—*home*—seemed to weigh heavily on all of them.

"You didn't fall, Buzz," Carter said. "The tree fell. And that was *my* fault."

Vanessa stared at each of the boys in turn. It was the closest thing to an apology she'd ever heard from Carter. Usually, he was too stubborn for anything like that. But then again, Carter had changed out here. They all had. And it seemed like the perfect time for some good news.

"Listen, you guys," she said. "First of all, it was stupid of me to run off like that. I'm really sorry, and I promise it won't happen again. But you're not going to believe what else happened. I found this cove up the shore. There's an old wrecked boat, and—"

Carter raised his head from where he lay in the sand. "What kind of boat?" he asked. Jane and Buzz sat up, too.

"I don't know," Vanessa said. "Not a sailboat. Some kind of ship. I didn't go on board."

"Why not?" Carter asked.

Vanessa paused. The real answer was because she'd found the grave and skeletal remains before she could explore the ship. But the whole point was to focus on positive news right now.

"Because I found a freshwater stream," she said. "And we don't have to go through those nasty caves to get to it, like the last one."

At that, all three of the others jumped up. The only fresh water they'd found until now was on the other side of a pitch-black maze of caves. Without any flashlight or torch to lead the way, it might as well have been on another island.

"Are you serious? Why didn't you say so?" Buzz asked.

"Let's go," Carter said. "Right now. I want to see this ship."

"I want a drink," Jane said.

"I want about eighteen drinks," Buzz said.

Vanessa stood and looked up the shore. It wasn't far to the cove, but it was tough going over that long stretch of volcanic rock. The others were already exhausted from their climb down.

Still, that didn't seem to matter, compared with the prospect of fresh water and supplies.

"All right, let's go," she said. "But just so you know, it's not going to be easy getting there."

Buzz had never explored the island's shore in this direction. None of them had, except for Vanessa. She was right about the slow going over the rocks, too. It took the better part of an hour to reach the cove.

But finally, he stood at the mouth of the wide inlet, staring at the big ship Vanessa had told them about.

It was strange, seeing anything man-made here. Anything from the outside world. The ship was maybe twice the length of the *Lucky Star*. That would make it a hundred feet long. The whole thing was grounded along its starboard side, at the far end of the cove.

"Where's the drinking water?" Carter asked.

Vanessa pointed past the bow of the ship. Behind it, water was seeping down a low, curved rock wall that formed the U-shape of the inlet itself. The stone was dark with moisture, and it was covered in the green moss and algae that seemed to grow everywhere in this quiet, shady spot.

All four of them—Jane, Carter, Buzz, and Vanessa— took off running. They splashed through shallow water, following the curve of the cove until they came to the stream at the back. It trickled down in several places. To get a drink Buzz pressed his face sideways against the mossy rock and let the cold water run into his mouth. It felt like suddenly waking up. Like a cool shower for his throat and insides.

For several long silent moments, nobody spoke. Carter and Jane had picked their own spots, where they gulped the water down in fast, loud sips. Vanessa stood back and waited for them to finish before she took her own drink.

Once he'd had his fill, Buzz turned his attention back to the boat. Its starboard hull loomed over the back of the cove like a giant metal wall. It looked as though it had been painted blue once, but most of it had gone to rust. A few black holes showed where the metal had corroded all the way through.

Five minutes ago, the idea of climbing up and exploring the ship had seemed overwhelming to Buzz. Now he was excited to see what they might find.

"Can we live here?" Jane asked.

"Why not?" Carter said. "It's huge. And the water supply's right here. We can't keep hiking back and forth over those rocks every time we need a drink."

Buzz liked the idea already. The boat would be dry, and there were probably real bunks on board. It also meant not having to rebuild their burned-out shelter. Trying to sleep on bamboo the last several nights had been like torture, anyway.

"Maybe we should look inside first," Jane said.

"Let's do it," Carter said, and started toward the ship.

"Actually," Vanessa said. "Hold on a second. There's something else you guys should see first."

Buzz looked at his sister. She had a strange expression on her face, but he couldn't tell what it was about.

"What kind of something else?" Carter asked.

Vanessa pointed over her shoulder, to a clearing in the woods. It sat at the top of the rock wall with the stream, and overlooked the whole cove. As for what might be up there, Buzz could only wonder.

But Vanessa seemed intent on showing them. Already, she was climbing up that way.

"Vanessa? What's going on?" he asked.

"Just come on," she said without looking back. "It's better if I show you."

***

Carter climbed up to the clearing behind Vanessa, Buzz, and Jane. It didn't take much effort, but by the time he reached it, all three of the others had stopped.

In fact, they'd gone perfectly still. And then Carter saw why.

Right there, stuck into the ground, was a handmade wooden cross. The wood was rough with age, just two cracked gray planks nailed together. There was no name, or markings of any kind.

"Is that a . . . grave?" he asked.

"I think so," Vanessa said. "And there's more. Don't freak out, but there's a bunch of bones over there—"

"What?" Buzz asked.

"Actually, not just bones," Vanessa said. "More like a skeleton."

Carter felt a chill run through him. He looked in the direction Vanessa had pointed, but he couldn't see anything.

She led them across the clearing and pulled back some low-hanging vines. What Carter saw there on the ground looked like some kind of movie prop, even though it clearly wasn't. He'd seen skeletons before, at the Museum of Science and Industry back home in Chicago.

This one was definitely real. It was half sunk into

the ground and mostly the color of dirt from however many years it had been here.

Jane reached over and took Carter's hand.

"Do you think there are more?" Buzz asked. "That's a big boat for two people."

"It's possible the others got rescued," Vanessa said.

"Or maybe there's more than one person buried under that cross," Carter said. He looked down at the skeleton again and shivered. "This guy was probably the last one."

"That's what I was thinking," Vanessa said. "There wasn't anyone left to . . . take care of him."

Only Jane stayed silent. She pulled her hand out of Carter's and knelt down by the remains. Slowly, she reached out and laid her fingers over the delicate hand bones of whoever this person had been.

"Don't touch it!" Vanessa said.

"Why not?" Jane asked. She kept her gaze down, and Carter could see the tears on her cheeks.

"Jane?" he asked.

"We were so close to being rescued," she said in a

faraway voice. "That plane . . . it was right there. And now . . ."

She didn't finish, but Carter knew what she was thinking. If these adults with their big ship had never gotten off the island, what did that mean for the four of them?

Carter's thoughts churned while the jungle hummed with the sound of a million bugs and birds all around them. Finally, he spoke up again.

"We need to get real about this," he said.

"What do you mean?" Vanessa asked him. "About what?"

He looked out toward the mouth of the cove, and beyond that, the bluest ocean any of them had ever seen. "That plane might have been our only chance," Carter said. "If they were looking for us, then they just crossed this place off their list—"

"You don't know that," Vanessa countered. "Besides, it's not the only plane out there. Beth and Dad are doing everything they can. You know they are."

"Hold on, Vanessa," Buzz said. "Carter's right. I mean, we should definitely build a new signal fire and make sure we're ready if another plane comes. But we need to think about what happens if . . ."

"If what, Buzz?" Vanessa asked stubbornly.

"If it never comes."

Buzz was crying now, too. They all were. Carter could feel the tears stinging at the corners of his eyes. A week ago, he might have tried to hide them, but it didn't seem worth it anymore.

"Why are you guys being like this?" Vanessa asked.

"We're not being like anything," Carter said. "It's just facts. There's nothing anyone can do for this guy, but we do need a place to live. And we can sure use his ship."

"Actually," Jane spoke up in a small voice, "there *is* something we can do for him."

Carter stopped and looked at her. Usually when Jane spoke up, it was for a good reason. "Like what?" he asked.

"We can give him a funeral," Jane answered. "The one he never had."

An hour later, Buzz stood back and looked at what they'd accomplished. It had been tough work—he was covered with sweat—but he was glad they'd listened to Jane.

The ground here was too rocky for digging, even if they'd had a shovel. Instead, they'd gathered all the big stones they could find and formed a mound over the skeletal remains. Jane said the mound was called a *cairn*, though she couldn't remember where the word came from. After the last of the rocks had been stacked, she'd picked several white and yellow flowers from the woods and placed them on top.

Now everyone stood around, shifting on tired feet. "Should we say something?" Buzz asked. It seemed like the right thing to do, but he wasn't sure what to say.

Then quietly, Jane started in.

"You died here alone, and nobody ever knew it," she said. She was facing the cairn and clearly speaking to whoever was inside. "Now we know it, and if we ever get out of here, other people will know it, too. Nobody's going to forget about you. That's a promise."

"Also, thank you for the ship," Vanessa said.

It was a strange thing to say, Buzz thought, but it also seemed right. He hadn't thought of anything to offer himself, although several questions had been running through his mind for the last hour.

What happened here? Why were these people never rescued? What had they done wrong?

Maybe the answer was . . . nothing. Maybe they'd done everything they could. But if they *had* made a mistake, Buzz thought, and if he and the others could figure out what it was, then maybe—just maybe— it could bring them a step closer to getting rescued themselves.

And if that happened, then maybe these people would have died for something. To help save the four of them.

Buzz realized *that* might be a nice thing to say, once he'd thought it. But the moment had passed. Carter, Jane, and Vanessa were already turning away, headed down to the ship.

It was time to get back to work.

CHAPTER 4

arter reached up with his good hand and pulled himself onto the deck of the abandoned ship. With the funeral behind them, his thoughts had turned back to whatever might be waiting for them on board.

Vanessa, Buzz, and Jane scrambled up behind him, and they worked their way toward the ship's two-level wheelhouse. It sat like a small building on the main deck, with doors on either side, port and starboard.

When Carter reached the port entrance, he saw at a glance how dead the place was inside. An instrument panel near the door was smashed and dented, its old glass gauges covered in a thick layer of grime. Vines grew in through the spaces where the windows used to be and ran in a tangle all around the room.

"I think this is communications over here," Vanessa said. The first thing on everyone's mind was the radio—but it didn't take long to rule out that possibility. Vanessa flipped several switches and turned a few levers, but nothing happened. It was all just junk by now.

Carter went straight up a set of steep metal stairs to find the captain's wheel on the top level. A dead clock above the broken-out windows had stopped at 10:35. There seemed to be some navigation equipment as well, but it was just as lifeless as everything else. He didn't see any paper charts, either.

"There's more stairs over here," Buzz's voice came from below, followed by a metal groan and echoing footsteps.

Then Carter heard Vanessa call out. "Buzz, slow down," she said. "Wait for me."

"Well, come on, then," Buzz answered back. "I think there might be—"

Whatever he said next was swallowed up by

another metallic groan, a loud snapping sound, and then an enormous crash.

Carter raced back down to the main level of the wheelhouse. Jane stood alone in an open hatchway at the back, looking into the space below. If any stairs had been there a minute ago, they were gone now. All Carter could see was the hole left behind and a cloud of gray dust.

"Buzz?" he shouted. "Vanessa?"

Vanessa struggled to catch her breath. The fall had knocked the wind right out of her. Buzz started coughing first. As the cloud of dust and particles cleared, she could see him on the floor, rubbing his head.

Her own first breath turned into a cough as well. She covered her mouth and hacked up a lungful of dust while Jane and Carter scrambled down to reach them. The ceilings were low here. It wasn't a far drop from the main deck to this one.

"Is everyone okay?" Carter asked.

"I think so," Vanessa said. She was getting used to being banged up in a way that she never would have shrugged off at home. They all were.

As the dust continued to clear, the space around them revealed itself. They were in a small plain room, with portholes on either side. There were two long tables with matching benches, and a line of framed maps on the wall, mostly with broken glass. A stack of wooden pallets sat in the corner. Vanessa recognized the gray, cracked planks right away. They matched the wood of the grave marker up in the clearing.

"We can use those for firewood," Carter said.

"And we can push one of these tables over," Vanessa said. "That'll make getting back out of here easier."

Working together, she and Carter dragged the collapsed staircase off to the side and pushed the nearest table into place, under the hatch door above.

From where they stood, narrow passages extended away in both directions. Toward the stern, Vanessa could see several open cabin doors.

"Here's the galley!" Jane called out from the other

direction. Immediately, Vanessa turned and followed the boys back that way to see.

It didn't take long to ransack the tiny kitchen and come up empty-handed. There were some pots and pans, and dozens of utensils, but that was it. Anything resembling a food locker was disappointingly empty. Whoever had been shipwrecked here before them had obviously gone through everything there was to eat. *Before they died,* Vanessa thought. It was depressing, but there was no use dwelling on it.

"Let's keep moving," she said, and peered down the corridor in the opposite direction. "What do you think's over there?"

Jane followed the others into the corridor that led toward the stern of the boat. There were two cabin doors on each side, all of them open.

"Everyone take a cabin," Carter said.

Jane turned and stepped over the raised sill of the doorway on her left. The tiny room looked more like an office than sleeping quarters. Besides a single porthole, the walls were covered with wire mesh shelving. A mess of old rotted cardboard boxes sat on some of the shelves. Others were piled in the corners. A quick look showed her they were all too stained and mildewed to be of any interest.

Jane turned her attention to the metal desk bolted against the wall. On the desktop, several old books sat in a stack, but the titles on their spines were written in an alphabet she didn't recognize. There was also a clear plastic paperweight with a sand dollar inside, and several empty metal cups. In one of the cups, she found a broken-off pencil, and immediately stuck it in her pocket.

On the wall over the desk was another framed map. Looking more closely, she saw that it was crisscrossed with longitude and latitude markings, and that several cities on the map were marked in English: Busan, Pyongyang, Seoul. It was the last one that Jane recognized.

"I think this ship is from Korea!" she called out to the others. She could see Carter across the hall, rooting through one of the sleeping cabins.

"Check it out!" he said. He held up a metal spool of some kind. "I think this is fishing line. And if we can find some wire, we can make hooks!"

It was a thrill, starting to unearth some of the ship's left-behind treasures. And its secrets, too.

Jane started opening desk drawers next, and she quickly found the one thing she'd most been hoping for. In the bottom left drawer, a stack of four leather-bound journals sat waiting for her. As she took them out and thumbed the yellowing pages, she saw more unfamiliar handwriting—Korean language, she supposed.

Best of all, each book had at least a few blank pages at the back. She could use those to restart her own journal, after losing the last one in the fire. It was tempting to sit down and start writing right away.

For the first several days on Nowhere Island, she'd recorded everything on video. It had begun as a report for her fifth-grade class. But after the shipwreck, it became more like a diary of life on the island.

When the camera's batteries ran down, she'd switched to writing by hand, in Uncle Dexter's captain's journal from the *Lucky Star*. Somewhere along the way, the journal became something else again—a way of not going crazy, maybe, or just a way to capture it all and hold it in one place.

Whatever it was, Jane hugged the journals to her chest, feeling happy for the first time in days. After a truly horrible morning, the afternoon was turning out to be much, much better.

Fresh water, a dry place to sleep, and a new journal. It wasn't a lot, but it sure felt that way.

"Hey, you guys!" Buzz shouted from his cabin down the hall. "Come look at this!"

He stood in one of the three sleeping chambers, staring at the floor. A manhole cover of some kind was sunk into the roughly textured metal deck. He'd seen several throughout the ship already, each one of them tightly bolted down.

Until this one.

Whoever had been here before had left it open for

some reason. Half a dozen loose bolts and an old rusted wrench lay on the floor nearby. Two more bolts were half screwed into their holes, holding the cover in place.

Vanessa appeared in the door. "What is it?" she asked. Carter was there now, too, and Jane squeezed between both of them to see.

"I don't know," Buzz said. "I was just going to find out."

He picked up the wrench and fitted it to the first bolt. It was stiff and took some effort, but soon it loosened right up. He was able to finish taking it out with just his fingers.

The same was true on the second one.

With the bolts removed, there was still the matter of prying the big steel disc out of its place in the floor. Carter, Vanessa, and Jane gathered around, and they all crammed their fingers into the small space the bolts had left behind.

"Ready?" Carter said. "One, two, three—"

Buzz heaved along with the others. The cover was snugly fitted. It seemed to have formed a seal over the hole, or whatever was down there. It took several tries before it came up even a fraction of an inch.

"Again!" Buzz said. "It's coming!"

They all lifted again. With a scrape of metal and the sound of sucking air, the cover finally came free. They shuffled it to the side, then let it drop onto the deck with a huge clang.

The next thing Buzz noticed was the smell. A harsh chemical odor poured up and out of the dark space beneath the floor.

Jane gagged. "What is that?" she asked.

"Oh, man!" Carter said, backing up. "Did we just open a sewer?"

"I don't think so," Buzz said. He lifted the collar of his T-shirt over his mouth and nose before he looked down inside.

Just below floor level, he could see the top of a ladder built into the side of whatever tank they'd just opened. An old stained rope was tied to the top rung and extended down into the darkness. For about the hundredth time in the last week, Buzz wished for a flashlight.

Instead, he reached down and grabbed hold of the

rope. It was greasy and also sticky in his hands as he started to pull.

"Buzz? What are you doing?" Vanessa asked.

There was some resistance on the line at first. Then it gave way all at once. A bucket appeared out of the black, hanging on the end of the rope. He could see it was filled with a thick, dark liquid of some kind.

Buzz's pulse quickened, thinking about what this might be. The others all stepped back while he lifted the full bucket up and out of the hole.

"What is it?" Jane asked.

"I think it's fuel," Buzz replied.

"Fuel?" Carter asked. "Like, gas?"

Buzz shrugged. He didn't know what these boats ran on. All he knew was that they'd just found something that *might* make life around camp easier. Which, in a place like this, was like striking gold.

Or maybe more like oil.

CHAPTER 5

For the rest of the afternoon, everyone kept busy, exploring their new home and bringing any useful items up onto the main deck. Jane catalogued it all in her journal, and everyone set to making what they could out of what they'd found.

Now, as the sun dipped to the west, Vanessa stood on the rocks at the mouth of the cove, dangling her homemade fishing pole in the water.

The pole wasn't much—a willowy branch from the woods, a piece of the plastic line Carter had found, and a wire she'd sharpened against the rocks to make a hook. With a snail for bait, she felt ready to catch some dinner.

Or more like desperate for it.

Up to now, Jane had proven herself to be the brain of the group. Buzz was the one who knew the most about survival, and Carter was the muscle. All Vanessa knew about herself anymore was that she was the oldest. It didn't seem to be adding up to much lately.

Nobody had said whether or not they wanted her to be the group leader anymore. Not since she'd run off that morning, before everything had gone so wrong.

And maybe that was for the best, Vanessa thought. Maybe they didn't need a leader anymore. What they needed right now was fish.

Back at the ship, she could see Buzz, busily working on the campfire. He'd brought up several bucketloads of sand to make a big fire pit right there on the ship's steel deck, surrounded by a ring of flat stones from the beach. It hadn't taken him long after that to find a broken glass bottle he could use to refract the sunlight and get a flame started, like he'd done before. Already, he had a good blaze going near the ship's bow.

Meanwhile, Carter was up in the woods, crashing around and scavenging for anything they could use, or eat. And Jane sat on a rock near the water's edge, scribbling away in her new journal.

"Any nibbles yet?" Jane asked, for what felt like the hundredth time.

"Not yet," Vanessa said. She was trying to be patient. It had been at least two hours, and she hadn't even gotten the tiniest pull on her line.

It was frustrating. They'd all been swimming in this water and seen a million fish just under the surface. But that was farther out, where the coral reef seemed to attract endless numbers of them.

The reef was where they needed to go, she thought. Somehow, they'd have to get themselves out onto the water. There was plenty of bamboo around. Maybe she could figure out how to make a workable raft.

But not today. The sun was already on its way down. It would be getting dark soon.

"I'm going in," she said to Jane. "Do you want to come back with me?"

Jane closed her journal, using her finger as a bookmark as Vanessa came near. "Not yet," she said. "I'm going to write a little more."

Vanessa looked to the horizon, where the sky had just started to dim. She could hear the bugs, warming up for their all-night chorus in the jungle. She could even smell the cool night air coming on.

It was all strangely familiar now, as if her senses had gotten sharper out here. She could spot the hermit crabs in the sand even when they weren't moving, and she swore she could tell the different calls of the cicada, the loudest insect she'd ever heard. Or maybe she was just imagining it.

She looked down at Jane again. "Don't . . ." she started to say, but then changed her mind and headed toward the ship.

"Don't what?" Jane asked after her.

"Nothing," Vanessa said. It was tempting to tell her not to stay out here too long. The mosquitoes always got worse around sunset, and it was important for the four of them to stick together after dark.

But Jane knew that. Even more, Jane could make

her own decisions around here. She'd proven that by now.

They all had.

———

Jane sat quietly, waiting until Vanessa had gone back to the ship. Then she opened her new journal and silently read what she'd written so far.

Dear Mom and Dad,

First of all, I'm not going to call you Mom and Eric anymore. Just Mom and Dad, if that's okay with you. I miss you both so much! I wish like anything you were here.

Wait. No, I don't. I wish WE were THERE . . .wherever you are. When I think about it, I like to imagine you on a plane, somewhere just out of sight. Like you're almost here to pick us up and take us home.

I probably shouldn't even think about that. It hurts when I do. But I also can't help it. I know you're out there—SOME-WHERE. And I know you're looking for us.

You'd probably want to know that we're taking care of each other. Vanessa's a really good older sister. I'm glad she's here with me. Buzz and Carter, too. I wish you could know that, because I'm sure you're worrying about us. You're probably even wondering if we're still alive.

Well, we are.

And we all love you.

And we MISS YOU. Huge, like the ocean.

xoxoxoxo, Jane (and Vanessa and Carter and Buzz)

P.S. If anyone finds this note, PLEASE send it to Elizabeth Benson and Eric Diaz at the address on the bottom of this page. It's more important than you can ever know. Thank you!

Jane carefully tore the page out of her journal. With another quick look back, she made sure she was still alone. Then she reached down between the rocks and pulled up the old bottle she'd found in a corner of the ship's galley. It smelled terrible on the inside but still had a screw cap to keep the whole thing watertight.

Standing with her back to the ship, she quickly rolled the letter into a tight scroll, slid it into the bottle, and sealed the whole thing up again.

It was stupid to throw a bottled note into the ocean. It was babyish, and impossible to think that the note might actually reach someone out there. If Carter, Buzz, or Vanessa knew she was doing it, they'd probably laugh her right off the island.

But none of that mattered. Above all, she kept thinking about something her mother liked to say. *If you don't try, you'll never know.*

It couldn't hurt, anyway. Even just writing the

letter felt good, like making a tiny connection to the real world back home.

Looking toward the horizon, Jane held the bottle in both hands. She gave it a quick kiss for good luck and threw it as far as she could. It splashed into the ocean, several yards offshore, and bobbed there, not going anywhere for the time being.

Jane watched for a few seconds more, then turned away and headed back to the ship. She'd done what she could. The rest was up to luck.

Carter stood perfectly still. *Don't move, Benson,* he told himself. *Not even so much as a twitch.*

It was dim in the woods. The sun had started to go down, and everything was washed in the pale blue color of dusk. But one thing stood out. It was the tan-and-black-banded snake, slithering off the tree in front of him.

It moved slowly off a low branch, taking its time. Carter wondered if the snake was aware of him or not. If so, it didn't seem to care. The thing had never seen a human before—that was for sure. It was just going about its business, heading for the carpet of leaves and brush on the forest floor.

Carter's heart raced with adrenaline, but there was no fear. He was too hungry for that. He'd heard of people eating rattlers before. Why not this one, too? It was at least three feet long, and thick. Which meant *meaty*, Carter thought. Its tiny black eyes were barely visible on either side of its flat, triangular head.

That was what he'd aim for—the head. But first, he needed a weapon.

Keeping his feet planted, he looked around for anything he could easily grab. A gray fist-sized rock sat in the weeds just a few feet away. It was smaller than he would have liked, but it would have to do. Moving slowly, he crouched down and picked up the rock with his good hand, never taking his eyes off the snake.

Now, he waited. The snake paused and advanced, paused and advanced, working its way toward the base of the tree trunk. Eventually, it slid onto flat ground, where it stopped again.

This was his chance. Any doubts he might have had were drowned out by the sharp, empty ache in his stomach. In one fluid motion, Carter dropped and brought the rock down on the snake's head with all the strength he had.

It was a direct hit. But the snake reacted with a speed of its own. Its tail and back half kicked up, coiling around Carter's leg. He felt a squeeze on his thigh as he jumped back. His fingers wrapped around the snake's leathery body, and he whipped it off his leg, dropping it to the ground again. Without pause, he stepped forward and pinned the thing with his sneaker.

For a full minute or more, the snake's body continued to move. It writhed under his foot, slowly curling and uncurling, until finally, it went still.

Carter looked down at his kill. He prodded it with his toe to make sure it was dead. Then he picked it up and turned to go.

It was only as he headed back to the ship that his

nerves started to kick in. His hand trembled as he walked, with the lifeless snake hanging in his grip. He realized he'd barely breathed the whole time, and his lungs worked to catch up.

I can't believe I just did that, he thought. Some animal part of him had taken over. It all happened in a blur.

But now, one thing was clear above all. He knew what was coming next.

Dinner!

CHAPTER 6

Other than microwave popcorn, Vanessa had never been much of a cook. But since Carter had made the kill, and Buzz was keeping the fire, she volunteered to do something with the snake. She only wished she could have brought back some fish to go with it.

Everyone was so hungry, there was no talk of how disgusting this might have been in any other situation. Not even from Jane, who could barely stomach the snails. Now, even she was excited at the prospect of something new to eat.

The first thing they had to do was use a knife from the galley to cut off the snake's head. Jane said that if the snake was venomous, that's where the poison would be. She didn't know what kind of snake it was, but offered that it looked like a boa of some kind.

"Looks like snake steaks to me," Carter said, and pitched the severed head way back into the woods. "The rats can have that part."

With the head gone, Vanessa was surprised at how easily the skin came off. It was like peeling a sock away from a long tube. It made sense, actually. Snakes were built to shed.

After that, everyone agreed that it was best to slit the whole thing open and clean out the insides, the same way they'd seen Joe Kahali clean fish on the *Lucky Star*. For that, Vanessa took the snake and climbed down to the water's edge. After she'd sliced it along the belly, all the insides pulled out in one long, slimy piece. If she weren't so hungry, that part alone would have made her sick, Vanessa knew. It was amazing how easily it came to her now. She dropped the innards in the water without a thought and climbed back onto the deck with the snake meat dangling in her hand.

"Let's cook this thing," she said.

Buzz already had a pot heating over the campfire. The pot sat on a broken metal frame that Carter had torn out of the nav station for a cooking grate. The whole setup was kind of pathetic-looking and brilliant at the same time.

Vanessa cut the meat into small pieces so they'd cook quickly. Within a minute of dropping them into the hot pot, the smell reached her nostrils, and her mouth started to water.

As soon as the pieces felt firm to the touch, she passed one out to each of them. She blew on hers, trying to cool it, but quickly lost patience and popped the hot little nugget into her mouth.

The meat was chewy and full of tiny bones, but nobody cared about that. Even the flavor, like a cross between unsalted fish and dark-meat chicken, tasted as good as anything Vanessa had ever eaten.

For a long time, nobody said much. There was plenty to eat, and they all dipped back into the pot for another piece, and another, and another. Nobody even counted or kept track of who was getting how much. For once, it didn't matter.

Finally, Vanessa sat back, amazed at the tight feeling in her belly.

"I can't believe it," she said. "I'm full."

"Me, too," Buzz said. "When was the last time that happened?"

"Best. Snake. Ever!" Jane said.

And when everyone laughed, it was a little bit like getting dessert, too.

After the snake was gone, Buzz had one more idea for the day. He'd gathered up a few supplies, and now pulled them out of the wheelhouse.

"What are you doing?" Carter asked. He, Jane, and Vanessa were stretched out around the fire, keeping warm as the cool of the night came on. A chilly breeze from the ocean blew around the deck, and a sky full of stars had started to show overhead.

"I want to make a torch," Buzz said. "If I can."

He picked up a long thin piece of firewood and a bag of old oil-stained rags he'd found in the engine room. The rags hadn't seemed good for anything at first. Not until this idea had come to him.

He wrapped a thick, triple layer of material around the top of the stick. Then he bound it up with a long piece of wire he'd pulled out of a dead console in the wheelhouse. It worked like metal string, which was exactly what he needed.

"And now, the secret ingredient," he said, grinning at the others. He turned the would-be torch upside down and dipped it into a pot of the dark, oily sludge from the tank they'd found.

"How do you know that's going to burn?" Jane asked him.

"I don't," he said. He swirled the cotton rags around and around, getting them good and soaked.

"How do you know it won't explode?" Vanessa added.

Buzz shrugged. "I don't."

The others stood up and took several steps away. Buzz set the oil-soaked head of the torch on the ring of stones around the fire. Then he stepped back, too. Using another stick, he slowly pushed the torch toward the flames. Jane put her hands over her ears. Buzz squinted, waiting for whatever might come next.

The fire burned bright orange all around the rags, but nothing happened. Buzz pushed the torch farther into the fire and waited again. Then, with a hollow popping sound, the whole thing quietly burst into flame.

Carter, Jane, and Vanessa erupted in a cheer.

"Sweet!" Carter said.

Buzz was already feeling high after a full meal. Now, a wide grin spread across his face. He'd done it.

He reached over and took the torch by its handle, stood up with it, and stepped away from the campfire. It burned on its own beautifully—a bright yellow beacon against the dark sky.

This was amazing. It was like holding a giant flashlight. It was security on a dark night. It was *power*. Not just for him but for all of them. Already, Jane, Vanessa, and Carter were picking up sticks of their own and starting to assemble more of the homemade torches.

Within a few minutes, everyone had one. It felt like the Fourth of July, with a warm glow lighting the deck of the abandoned ship.

"Come on," Buzz said. "Let's test these things out."

"Where are you going?" Jane asked.

"For a walk."

Buzz went to the ship's rail and dropped his torch onto a dry patch of ground below. It hit the dirt and kept right on burning.

Soon all four of them were off the boat, headed toward the mouth of the cove. The torches lit the way as they climbed out onto the rocks to look at the endless stars and bright half-moon overhead.

Buzz could feel the warmth of the flames on his face. It was an amazing sensation—and, strangely, one of the most secure feelings he'd ever had.

"I think we can do this, you guys," he said.

"Do what?" Vanessa asked.

He gestured, sweeping his arm at the ocean, the shore, the cove—all of it.

"This," he said.

For a moment, no one said anything. They all

seemed to be taking in the power of the idea. They could do this. They *were* doing this.

Vanessa was the first to break the silence. "What do you think Dad and Beth would think if they could see us now?" she asked.

"You don't have to call her Beth," Jane said. "You can call her Mom. I bet she'd like that."

"I'll bet you're right," Vanessa said. For once, nobody seemed sad at the mention of their parents. "So what do you think Mom and Dad would think if they saw us now?"

"They'd think we were wild animals," Carter said, and let out a howl.

Then Buzz joined in. Jane and Vanessa, too. Soon, all four of them were laughing and baying at the moon, making as much noise as they pleased.

Why not? Buzz thought. This was *their* island, after all.

CHAPTER 7

When Carter woke up the next morning, rain was beating heavily against the cabin's porthole. That was no surprise. The weather changed all the time around here.

The surprise was that he could see daylight outside. Back at the old camp, sleeping in a cave at first, and then in their palm-and-bamboo shelter, none of them had ever gotten a full night's sleep. To actually wake up in the light, feeling rested, was amazing.

Now, Carter sat up and took a moment to check his hand. The cut from the base of the pinkie to his wrist was caked with dried blood. Even worse, it oozed yellow liquid around the edges. The hand itself was swollen, and he couldn't fully bend or straighten his fingers anymore. When he tried, the painful throb pulsed like a heartbeat in his hand.

Vanessa, Buzz, and Jane had all been telling him to keep the cut clean. But that was nearly impossible when your days were spent foraging in the jungle, cutting firewood, and moving all around an old, dirty ship. The sock he'd been using as a makeshift bandage had quickly grown so filthy, he'd thrown it away.

Carter stumbled out of the sleeping cabin and up the passageway to the center room outside the galley. Jane, Vanessa, and Buzz were sitting around the old wooden table, underneath the hatch that led up to the wheelhouse.

"Carter, your hand!" Vanessa said before he even spoke.

Carter shoved the hand into his pocket. He hadn't realized how obvious it would be.

"It feels fine," he said.

It was a lie, but if there was nothing they could do about it, there was no reason to worry everyone. They already had plenty to worry about. Vanessa narrowed her eyes at him, but Buzz spoke up before she could say anything else.

"We were talking about going to the old camp to get our stuff," Buzz said.

"Good idea," Carter said, glad for the change of subject. All of their things were still back there, including blankets, pillows, raincoats, and the axe.

"I think we should try to go through the woods," Vanessa said. "There's no way we can carry that stuff back over the rocks. And once we have a path, it'll probably be faster, too."

"The only question is whether we should wait for the rain to stop or just go," Jane said.

Carter looked at one of the dining hall portholes. It was so blurred with rain, he couldn't even see outside. Experience had shown them that this could be a passing shower, or it could continue all through the day.

"I say let's go for it," he said. "So we get wet, who cares? At least there's coconut back at camp."

"And coconut's way better than snails," Jane said.

Buzz nodded in agreement. "It's better than sitting around, too," he said.

That alone was a good enough reason to go, Carter thought. The hardest times here were at night, or whenever they stopped moving and working. That was when the dark thoughts tended to creep in the most.

"All right, it's decided then," Vanessa said, and stood up with the rest of them. "Let's go get wet."

The trip through the jungle was exactly as Jane expected. The rain poured down through the trees, and the ground was thick with mud in several places.

Even so, it was a shortcut compared to the rocky shoreline. Before long, they were slogging out of the woods and onto the beach they'd known as home base since crashing into the island a week ago.

There was no worrying about keeping dry anymore. In fact, being wet and muddy had become a badge of honor. It was how they lived here. They sat right down in the sand and opened two coconuts for a quick breakfast while the rain continued to fall.

As soon as they'd eaten, everyone agreed to gather up what they could, turn around, and head right back. Using their two blankets as packs, they piled in the axe, the sharp knife, the pillows, and all the remaining coconuts they could carry. There were four rain slickers as well, and everyone put one on.

Jane made sure to take the two pens she'd stashed between the rocks. Buzz took the little glass lens he used for making fire. He'd already found a substitute, but the old one was their good-luck charm, he said.

By the time they were loaded up and ready to go, the rain had gotten even worse. It poured down around them now like walls of water.

"Maybe we should wait," Jane said.

"Wait for what?" Carter asked.

Mother Nature had an answer for that question as she rocked the island with a massive bolt of lightning and a thunderous boom.

"What about the cave?" Jane asked.

"What about it?" Carter answered. "Remember

what happened the last time we used it to get out of a storm?"

Jane did remember. There was no forgetting that stampede of wild boars that had knocked her down— and very nearly done worse.

"If we're looking for shelter, so are they," Buzz added.

"Besides, Buzz already marked the trail," Vanessa said. "We can get back to the ship in fifteen minutes."

"But . . ." Jane started to protest, until she realized no one was listening anymore.

Carter slung one of the improvised blanket packs over his back. Vanessa took the other. Buzz carried the two coils of rope, one on each shoulder, and a pillowcase stuffed with silverware, socks, and some old sea charts from the *Lucky Star*.

Finally, Jane bent down and picked up the group's one backpack, filled with their water bottles, while the others glared at her impatiently.

They'd always babied her up till now, but not anymore. It didn't feel the way she'd always wanted it to, being treated just like anyone else. It felt scary.

But that was beside the point, wasn't it? Sometimes out here you had to accept what was and deal with it.

"Okay, I'm ready," Jane declared. "Let's go." She firmed her grip on the pack, wiped the rain out of her eyes, and started following the others back up into the woods.

CHAPTER 8

Mud sucked at Vanessa's feet as they made their way through the jungle. The heavy rain had turned the ground even muckier since they'd come through before. In the thickest patches, each step felt like lifting a heavy weight.

Their awkward load of supplies didn't help. It made maneuvering around the thick vines, over fallen trees, and under low branches that much more difficult. Several times, Vanessa had to stop and adjust the bundle on her back, or pick up something that had fallen out.

Buzz's blazed trail was the one thing that made the

going easier. He'd cut deep V-shaped gouges into the trees along the way, pointing them back toward the ship. Every ten or twenty yards, there was another blaze they could follow.

As they came onto a steep patch of ground where the land sloped toward the ocean, Vanessa stopped at the head of the line.

"What is that?" she asked, peering through the rain. Straight ahead, a heavy stream that hadn't been there before was washing downhill. It came from high on the slope to their left and continued all the way down to the ocean, somewhere off to the right. Most significantly, it ran directly across their path.

"Can we keep going?" Jane asked.

Buzz looked up and down the hill. "Do we have a choice?" he asked.

"We could go back if we have to," Vanessa said.

"And then what?" Carter said. "Carry all this stuff over the rocks? Leave it behind? I don't think so."

Nobody argued with that. Vanessa could tell they were all as anxious to reach the ship as she was.

"All right," she said. "Everyone hold on to each other. And be careful."

Vanessa took one end and locked arms with Buzz. He had Jane on the other side, with Carter at the opposite end. It was awkward going as they waded in, but it was better than trying to forge the gully separately. The water rushed by at a surprising speed, and the ground underneath was mush.

Vanessa lifted one foot and then the other, picking up her knees with each step. Her makeshift pack was soaked now and twice as heavy. She struggled to hold on to it with her outside hand.

"I don't know if I can carry this," she said.

"Just keep going," Carter said.

On the next step, Vanessa's foot landed in an unseen hole. Her leg sank deeper than ever, all the way up to her waist. When she tried to pull herself out, the mud at the bottom sucked her sneaker right off.

"Wait! I lost my shoe!" she yelled over the rain.

Buzz had been trying to keep hold of her arm, but now they'd been torn apart. Carter stumbled forward, too. He grasped his own pack with two hands and heaved it onto the ground at the far side of the gully. As soon as he did, he yelled out in pain and clutched his bad hand close to his chest.

"Carter? Are you okay?" Jane asked, but he didn't answer.

"Vanessa, here!" Buzz said, and reached to take her pack from her. As she handed it over, the knotted blanket came undone. One pillow and several precious coconuts washed downhill, immediately out of reach. Buzz threw the rest onto the bank.

"We have to go!" Jane yelled.

"I need my shoe!" Vanessa yelled back. She reached down, feeling for it, but found only handfuls of mud.

"It has to be there," Buzz said, his voice edged with impatience.

"I'm trying," Vanessa said. She knew they had to go, but a shoe wasn't something you could do without so easily around here.

Then, looking up, Vanessa saw something that erased all of her other concerns. A giant wall of mud had begun rolling downhill. It was headed toward them at an alarming rate.

"Vanessa!" Jane screamed. She'd seen it, too. Everyone had. Buzz started pulling on the group to get them going again.

"Leave the shoe!" he yelled. "Let's go!"

Vanessa couldn't move. She'd sunk too far now. She had no leverage to get herself out of the hole anymore. Buzz was straining, pulling on her arm, getting nowhere. Carter tried for her, but his hand was just out of reach.

They were running out of time, and the earth itself, it seemed, was pouring down in their direction.

***

Jane screamed.

"Watch out!" she yelled. Before she could move out of the way, a heavy wave of earth, mud, water, and debris smashed into them. She was caught in it now. They all were. The last she saw of the others, Vanessa's head had disappeared under the deluge, and Carter had lunged for the bank. She saw Buzz fall sideways, carried downhill by the mud itself.

It was the same for her. Everything was a blur at first, and then dark. There was no controlling her movement, or the direction in which she traveled. She tumbled along, as if in slow motion, half buried by the sludge.

Unseen rocks and roots thumped at her body. The trees on either side seemed to be traveling in the opposite direction. She reached for the bank, but it was impossible to move toward it.

Her mind raced. Would she be dumped into the ocean to drown? Buried alive? There was no knowing where this was taking her, or what would happen before it was over.

The mudslide had her, and there was nothing she could do about it.

Buzz couldn't see. He couldn't hear. He could only feel himself sliding downhill, carried along beyond his own control.

But then he sensed a change. The flow slowed. The

earth around him seemed to churn, and then came to a stop. It left him suspended where he was like any other piece of debris in the muck.

Muscles straining, Buzz struggled to get free. First, he managed to come onto his knees. He wiped away what he could from his eyes and then lunged toward the nearest bank. He was crawling more than walking, but it got him up onto higher ground.

Standing on shaky legs, he looked around.

"Vanessa!" he screamed. "Jane! Carter! Where are you?"

He'd lost all track of them. He had no idea if they were uphill, downhill, or still buried under the river of mud.

The first one he saw was Carter, lying on the same side of the gully, twenty or thirty yards uphill. He was on his back, panting heavily with his hand clutched to his chest.

"Vanessa! Jane!" Buzz yelled again.

"I'm here!" Jane's voice came from somewhere below. Buzz looked, but he couldn't see her through the woods.

"Are you okay?" Carter yelled.

"I . . . I think so," Jane called back. "I'm coming up."

"Where's Vanessa?" Buzz asked. His heart thumped like a fist in his chest. "Carter, do you see her?"

Carter sat up to look around. "No!" he called.

The last Buzz had seen Vanessa, she was stuck in a hole, somewhere uphill of this spot, but nothing looked familiar anymore. The mudslide had completely disoriented him.

He worked his way higher, struggling to hurry. With the heavy mud on his arms, legs, and clothes, he felt as if he were running underwater.

"Vanessa!" he yelled again.

And then he saw her. Vanessa's arm was sticking out of the mud in the middle of the gully, reaching and flailing for something to grab on to. The rest of her was completely submerged.

"Get her!" Carter shouted. Jane was coming up behind them now, and they rushed toward the spot.

How much time had passed? One minute? Two minutes? All Buzz knew right now was that Vanessa was still moving. And he had to get her out, whatever it took.

Without hesitation, he launched himself back into the gully. Quickly, the mud was past his knees and putting a hard grip on him. Another few steps and he'd be part of the problem instead of the solution.

But Vanessa was still out of reach. Panic was setting in. It was hard to think of what to do.

"Buzz, she's going to suffocate!" Jane yelled.

"No, she's not!" Buzz said. There was no way he'd let his sister go down like this. It wasn't going to happen. The truth of it burned into his gut. "Get me something!" he yelled back. "The axe, or a branch—anything!"

Jane and Carter were on it right away. "Here!" Jane handed him a long crooked branch. It whipped Buzz in the face as he turned to take it, but he barely noticed.

He reached out now, swinging the tree limb in Vanessa's direction.

"Vanessa! HERE!" he yelled as loudly as he could. Whether or not she could hear him, he had no idea. Her hand swung from side to side, sweeping the air until it finally struck the branch. Then her fingers closed around it.

"Now pull!" Carter said to Buzz from behind. Buzz could feel Jane's and Carter's hands around his waist, yanking on him and doing what they could to help.

Vanessa held tightly to the opposite end of the branch, but the suction of the mud was so tight, it threatened to pull Buzz in after her. He dug his heels into the sludge and held on. Then he managed a single step back. Then another.

Slowly, the top of Vanessa's head emerged. Her other arm came out of the muck, and she grabbed the branch with both hands now. Buzz gripped his end as hard as he could, while Jane and Carter guided him backward. When he hit the bank, he stumbled and fell right onto Jane.

As Vanessa's head cleared the mud, her face was still completely covered. Her lips parted, and she took a huge gasp of air, even as more mud dropped into her mouth. She spit and coughed, then spit again, and finally took a full breath. Buzz leaned forward and grabbed on to her as she clawed her way toward the bank.

Finally, he fell back again, catching his own breath. His strength was gone, his muscles like rubber. He'd poured out everything he'd had, and then some. But everyone was safe now. That's what mattered most.

When he looked up, Vanessa was still sheathed in mud. The skin on her face was sagging under the weight. She looked eighty years old, at least.

And Buzz started to laugh. He couldn't help it. His thirteen-year-old sister looked more like their great-grandma Diaz than herself right now.

"What are you laughing at?" Vanessa gasped out.

Buzz put his arms around her and let the rain pour down, washing them clean.

"Nothing," he said. "I'm just glad you're okay."

"I lost my shoe," Vanessa said weakly.

That only made Buzz laugh harder. He couldn't stop. It wasn't just the shoe. It was the sense of relief. For a moment, he'd thought they might actually lose Vanessa. And that had been too much to bear.

Finally, they stood up again and started gathering what they could. Buzz threw several provisions into one of their soaking-wet blankets, tied it into a bundle, and picked it up, feeling ready to get back to the ship once and for all.

He turned to where Carter had been standing and doing nothing for the last minute. "Can you take this?" Buzz asked, holding out the bundle for him.

Carter nodded, reached for it, and then dropped the pack as soon as he tried to take it.

"Carter?" Jane said. "What's wrong?"

Carter's expression was a twist of pain. "My hand," he said. It was bleeding again. His fingers were curled and swollen, and his face was pale as he looked around at the group. "I don't think I can use it anymore."

CHAPTER 9

July 9. Day 11 on Nowhere Island. Two weeks(!!) since we left Hawaii.

Dear Mom and Dad,

It seems like forever since I saw you. I know these letters aren't real, but I like writing them anyway.

It's been three days since the mud-slide, and we haven't been able to get back to the old camp since then. Not even along the rocks.

The problem is, our old beach is where the coconuts grow. We've been all over the woods around here and haven't found a single one. No other fruit, no nuts, no nothing. Not even another snake. The one thing we have left to eat here is snails. And you know how I feel about those! Still, I eat them, and it feels like nothing in my stomach. You should see how different we all look now. I think maybe we're starting to starve, for real.

Vanessa's working really hard trying to catch fish, but I don't think they want to be caught. She thinks maybe if we build a raft, we can get out to the reef and find more of them there. So far, we've cut down a bunch of bamboo from the woods (too bad we can't eat bamboo), and we work on the raft a little bit every day. It's hard to get much done with just a few snails for breakfast, lunch, and dinner.

I know we'll figure something out, but I really (really, REALLY) wish we would hurry up and do it. All we think about is food these days. I shouldn't even be writing this right now. I should be getting ready to go out into the woods and start looking before the sun gets too high.

Maybe this will be our lucky morning. I hope so.

Miss you, love you,

xoxoxoxo to infinity,

Jane

Buzz knelt down next to Carter's bunk and put a hand on his arm. Carter's skin was hot to the touch. He definitely had a fever, and he'd been sleeping more than anyone.

"Carter?" Buzz shook him gently. "We're going out scavenging. Can you come up and watch the fire?"

Carter stirred and came half awake. "I wanna come hunting," he slurred.

"We need someone to watch the fire," Buzz repeated. It wasn't totally true. On a sunny day like this one, Buzz could easily use his little glass lens to restart the fire. In fact, he'd gotten really good at it. But everyone agreed that Carter needed to rest as much as possible.

Carter sat up and stretched. "I'll go out and get some wood, at least," he said.

"Already did it," Buzz told him. "There's a ton of it in the wheelhouse. Just make sure the fire doesn't go out. There's a bucket of oil up there, too, if you need it. And I left some water. Make sure you drink a lot."

It was strange, telling Carter what to do. Not that long ago, it had been the other way around most of the time.

But Carter didn't argue. "I'll be right there," he said.

Buzz left him in the cabin and walked up the passage to the middle deck's central room. From there, he climbed onto the table, stepped onto the steel trunk they'd found in one of the cabins, and climbed up through the hatch to the wheelhouse above. It was enough of a makeshift stairs that even Carter could do it with one hand. But for how much longer, Buzz wasn't sure. That hand wasn't getting any better. The only thing they could do now was try to get some food into Carter, to keep up his strength.

And *that* was proving harder than anyone had thought it would be.

Inside the wheelhouse, Buzz picked up the axe and the backpack they used for scavenging. The pack was loaded with a sharp knife, a length of rope, and two empty bottles they'd fill at the stream on their way out.

Stepping outside, he could see Jane down by the water's edge, writing in her journal. Vanessa was there, too, looking down at a row of bamboo she'd been trying to puzzle into a raft.

And out by the ocean, at the mouth of the cove, Buzz could see their new signal fire. He liked looking at it. It was the one thing that had come together well in the last three days. The tall tepee-shaped pyre of wood and kindling was similar to the signal they'd had on Lookout Point. It didn't have the advantage of being up high like the last one, but if another plane or a ship came by, they could at least get to this one to light it in a matter of seconds.

"You guys ready to go?" Buzz called down to the girls.

Jane stood up and closed her journal. "What are we looking for today?" she asked.

"Cheeseburgers," Vanessa answered. It was a daily joke now. The day before it had been pizza, and the day before that, chocolate cake.

"Think we'll find any?" Vanessa added.

"Probably," Buzz said. "But we'd better get moving before they run out."

Vanessa led Jane and Buzz into the woods, hacking at anything that stood in their way. It wasn't necessary to take out quite so much brush, but the entire jungle was getting on her nerves today.

The air here was a thick stew of humidity and stillness. It was like breathing through a wet washcloth. The shoes she'd borrowed from Carter for the morning were too tight, and the mosquitoes were always terrible in the woods. She didn't even bother trying to wave them off anymore. There was no point.

She stopped and scanned the area, hoping for a flash of color that might turn out to be something edible. Bananas would have been amazing, or papaya, or mango, or any of the other things Jane said grew in this part of the world. Even coconut or another snake would have been more than welcome. But so far all they'd brought back from these morning hikes was firewood and kindling.

"Can we burn this?" Jane's voice came from the other side of a scraggly thicket.

"What is it?" Vanessa asked. She ducked under a tangle of vines and worked her way over to where Buzz and Jane were looking down at a large dead tree on the ground.

"We could get a lot of firewood out of this," Jane said.

"Does rotten wood burn?" Vanessa asked. She put one foot on the tree and buried the axe blade into its bark three times. On each swing, it landed with a soft thud that didn't sound too encouraging. The wood only broke open and fell apart where she tried to cut it.

"Come on, let's keep going," Vanessa said.

"Wait!" Buzz said. The excitement in his voice stopped her. She turned back to see him kneeling right on top of the tree.

"What is it?"

"Jane, hand me the knife," Buzz said. Already, he was picking through the crumbly bark with his fingers. Jane opened the pack on his back and handed him a six-inch serrated blade. He took it and plunged the tip into the soft wood, working the knife around in circles to open up a hole.

Whatever Buzz was doing, Vanessa could see he was onto something. His eyes were still and focused, his mouth set in a frozen line of concentration. Before Nowhere Island, the only time she'd seen that expression was when Buzz sat on the couch at home, deep inside a game of FarQuest or Reverb Alley.

"What are you doing?" Vanessa asked.

"I thought I saw a grub," Buzz said.

"A what?"

He withdrew the knife now and stuck two fingers inside. When he pulled them out, he had a pinch hold on a lumpy white worm the size of his pinkie.

Buzz dropped it onto his palm and held the thing out to show them. "These little suckers are pure protein," he said.

Jane leaned in to see. "We're supposed to eat *those*?" she asked.

"I'm not saying they're candy bars," Buzz told her. "I'm just saying they're edible. And there's probably a lot more of them here, too."

The grub was more like a caterpillar than a worm, Vanessa realized. It had a shiny dark head at one end and tiny legs that sent it wriggling across Buzz's palm. Snails were one thing, but the grub was ten times as big and probably twice as disgusting.

Her empty stomach seemed to fold in on itself. She knew exactly what she had to do, and she didn't like the answer one bit. It was another *island moment*. That's how Vanessa thought of them now.

She was going to eat grubs. Not because she liked

them. Not because she thought it would be fun. But simply because there was one thing about them that mattered more than anything else.

They were edible.

CHAPTER 10

Carter startled himself awake.

He'd been dreaming—about what, he wasn't even sure. Something had been chasing him. Something getting closer. Reaching out to grab him. And then—

He sat up on the deck, breathing heavily and remembering where he was. This fever wasn't doing him any favors—that was for sure.

The campfire had burned down while he slept. Its embers were still bright orange, but he needed to feed it soon if he didn't want to lose it. With Buzz, Vanessa, and Jane off sweating in the jungle, it was the very least he could do.

Carter shuffled across the deck and into the wheelhouse for more of the dry wood Buzz had stacked there. His bad hand was swollen stiff, but he could still grip certain things like pieces of firewood, as long as they weren't too small. He bent down, grabbed an armload, and stood up.

His head swam. The room started spinning. Carter dropped the wood, leaned against the wall, and slid back down to the floor.

Tears squeezed out from the corners of his eyes. Even standing too fast was a problem. It was beyond frustrating. When they'd landed on the island, he had been the strong one. He had been the one they could all count on to get the most done. But not anymore.

Without thinking, he pounded the steel deck with his bad hand. It sent a nauseating bolt of pain up his arm, and he screamed—as much from the frustration as anything else. He took up a piece of the firewood with his good hand and flung it as hard as he could, not caring where it went.

A small crash sounded from the other side of the room, followed by the sound of broken glass falling onto the floor. Carter looked over to see a row of framed photographs above the wheelhouse windows. Two of them were smashed, their frames splintered at the corners.

He'd walked by those photos a hundred times without ever really noticing them. Now he saw that they were fishing pictures. In one, several men were casting off the back of a boat. In another, someone stood on a dock next to an enormous swordfish.

It was a painful reminder of Carter's own empty belly and everything he hadn't been able to accomplish here. He picked up another piece of wood and took out two more of the photos with one throw.

For a long time, Carter didn't move. The anger that coursed through him was a paralyzing feeling. His muscles and his mind seemed locked up together inside of it. And who was there to blame for all this? *No one.* Not even himself.

They'd done nothing wrong. This was all supposed to have been a fun sailing trip, a week on the boat with Uncle Dexter. Their parents thought it would be a chance for the four kids to get to know one another better, as brothers and sisters. Now, here they were, fighting for their lives instead. And it sure didn't feel like a fair fight.

Slowly, Carter's thoughts evened out. He remembered what he had to do. He took his time standing up, gathered another armload of wood, and headed for the door.

He was nearly outside when he stopped again. Something about the fishing photos had caught his attention. One of them was different than the others, and he stepped back for a closer look.

The picture was an underwater shot. It showed a man in swim trunks, holding a spear of some kind. Instead of gripping the spear near the base like a regular weapon, the man held it near the barbed tip, with a long strap stretched all the way along its length. The whole thing seemed to be cocked like a slingshot, ready to fire.

It was nothing Carter had ever seen before, but as he looked at it, the spear made perfect sense. Vanessa had been talking about making a raft to get them out to the reef for fishing. It was a good idea, but what if they could get *down* to the reef as well? That's where the fish really were, after all.

Carter went outside and stoked the campfire, then jumped off the ship and headed straight up into the jungle. Vanessa had been harvesting bamboo for the raft, and he went right to the grove she'd told him about.

When he got there, he scouted out a long thin piece. It was nearly six feet high where it grew. Perfect for what he had in mind. Using his good hand he grabbed hold of the cane, angled his foot against the base, and snapped it free.

Back at the ship, he reentered the wheelhouse. There, he turned his attention to the row of windows at the front of the room. Most of them had broken or missing glass, but they all still had the black rubber weather stripping that ran around their frames. When he poked at the material with his finger, it seemed spongy, and maybe even stretchy enough for the job. He reached up and peeled away one of the strips, being careful to keep it all in one piece.

Already, Carter felt completely exhausted. He knew

he didn't have much more in him, but he wanted to get this done.

With the bamboo wedged between his knees, he looped one end of the rubber strip around its base and used his teeth to grab the other end, cinching it tight. He repeated the process, tying it off with one of the knots Uncle Dexter had taught him on board the *Lucky Star*. Now he had a big lasso of rubber attached to the end of his would-be spear.

There was just one more step, maybe the most important one. He grabbed one of the sharp knives and whittled away the tip of the bamboo until he'd created a strong, sharp point.

Even in his feverish state, Carter felt just a little bit better. The others had been working hard while he'd slept next to the fire. But now, in less than half an hour, with just the materials he had on hand, he'd worked up a pretty good fishing spear. It was simple and crude, but if it worked, it would change everything. They wouldn't have to starve, because they'd be drowning in fish.

The only thing left to do was test it out. But not

right now. As much as he wanted to keep going, Carter's swimming head and fuzzy thoughts told him otherwise. Reluctantly, he took some more wood out to the fire and lay down to close his eyes for a quick rest.

Just a few minutes, Carter thought. Then he'd be right back at it.

When Buzz got back to the ship with the girls, Carter was up on the main deck, dozing next to the campfire. It looked as if he hadn't moved from his spot in hours.

He sat up and rubbed his eyes as they all set down their armloads of fresh firewood.

"Any luck?" Carter asked.

"Well, the good news is, we found something to eat," Buzz said.

"What's the bad news?"

Buzz reached into his pocket and set down a handful of grubs.

"Say hello to our lunch."

Vanessa laughed nervously, Jane didn't say a word, and Carter leaned in for a better look. There were eighteen of them in all. A few of the grubs had died on the way, but most of them were wriggling around, trying to get back on their feet.

Buzz plopped down next to Carter, as did Jane and Vanessa.

"What are they?" Carter asked.

"You mean besides totally disgusting?" Jane asked. "They're grubs. Buzz says they're pure protein."

Buzz couldn't help feeling a little proud. Maybe the grubs *were* the grossest possible food source, but it was better than the alternative: no food at all.

"Who wants to go first?" he asked.

"I think you do," Vanessa said.

It was hard to argue with that. "Yeah, all right," he said. He picked one up and stared at it. The grub fidgeted back and forth between his fingers.

This is food, he told himself. *Nutrition. Protein. The stuff my body needs.*

Before he could think about it another second, he stuck the whole thing in his mouth and bit down hard. It sent a thick greenish liquid spilling over his lips and down his chin.

"EWWWW!" all three of the others groaned at once.

"*That* . . . is the grossest thing I've ever seen," Jane said.

Buzz knew he couldn't stop now. He tilted his head back, fighting the urge to spit the whole thing out. The grub tasted like dirt and chemicals. It didn't help that it was so chunky, either. But he kept on chewing, as fast as he could.

Finally, with one very hard gulp, it went down. He opened his mouth and stuck out his tongue to show he'd done it.

"I can't believe you just ate that," Carter said.

"It wasn't so bad," Buzz lied, and downed half a bottle of water to wash away the taste. He could still feel bits and pieces on his tongue, but he tried not to think about that. "Who's next?" he asked.

"Go ahead, Vanessa," Carter said. "I dare you."

"I dare *you*," Vanessa said.

Carter picked up two of the grubs and held them out on his palm.

"Let's race," he said.

Vanessa grinned uneasily as she took one from him. "Yeah, all right."

"Ready?" Jane asked. "One . . . two . . . three!"

Buzz watched as Vanessa tossed the grub onto her tongue, clapped both hands over her mouth, and started chewing.

"Carter!" Jane said. "That's even . . . grosser!"

When Buzz looked over, Carter was unclenching his fist. His hand was covered in pieces of squished grub and the greenish liquid. He held it up to his mouth, scraped the mess off with his teeth, and swallowed it all in one pass.

"Hey!" Vanessa said. "That's not fair!"

"Says who?" Carter asked. As if to make his point, he scooped up a second grub, squeezed it into a mush, and got it down before Vanessa had finished her first. All without a sip of water.

It wasn't such a bad idea, Buzz thought. At least it got rid of the need for any chewing. He picked one up for himself, closed his eyes, and squeezed. A soft, warm goo filled his hand, but he didn't look at it. He kept his eyes closed and downed the whole thing as quickly as possible. His stomach churned as he reached for the water bottle.

Vanessa was still struggling with her first one, but now that she'd started, she seemed determined to get through her share. She took a swig of water, picked up another grub, and kept going.

The whole time, Jane watched them as if she were sitting in front of a horror movie. Her hands never came down from her mouth, until finally, she scooted forward and looked down at the remaining wriggling grubs on the deck.

"What do you think, Jane?" Carter asked. His grin showed several little legs still stuck in his teeth, but he didn't seem to mind. In fact, the change in him was amazing. With even just a tiny bit of food, he was more alert than he'd been all day.

"Mom always says you should try everything once," he added. "I'll even mash it up for you."

"Don't bother," Jane said. She took a thin stick from the pile of kindling near the fire. Then she skewered three grubs, one by one, and held them over the glowing embers to roast. They looked like the world's ugliest marshmallows.

Buzz glanced at Carter and Vanessa, who looked back at him. It wasn't the first time Jane had proven herself to be the smartest one in the group.

Soon, everyone had a skewer going. Green liquid dripped and sizzled into the fire while the grubs roasted away. Buzz wasn't convinced this would make them taste any better, but one thing was for sure. They couldn't taste any worse.

"Good idea, Janie," Vanessa said.

"I'm going to pretend it's cooked fish," Jane said grimly. "And I don't even like fish."

"Oh—I almost forgot!" Carter said suddenly. He handed his skewer to Vanessa and walked toward the wheelhouse.

"Where are you going?" Vanessa called out.

"I have something to show you guys," he said. "I'll be right back."

As soon as Carter came out of the wheelhouse carrying his invention, Jane knew what it was.

"That's a Hawaiian sling!" she said. She abandoned

her skewer of grubs and went over for a closer look.

"It's just a spear," Carter said.

"Yeah—a *fishing* spear," she said. "Why didn't you tell us?"

Her brother shrugged. "I was pretty out of it when you got here."

"How does it work?" Vanessa asked.

Carter held up the black-and-white photograph he'd found and passed it around.

"Ohh," Buzz said, looking at the photo. "Sling, like slingshot. I get it."

He fitted the lasso around his elbow and pulled the bamboo shaft back until he was holding the spear close to the tip, like the man in the picture. The rubber loop stretched tight along its length.

Next, he moved over to the ship's rail and took aim. "Be careful!" Vanessa said, just before the spear sprang out of his hand. The whole thing flew toward the beach and stuck in the sand several inches deep. For a piece of bamboo and rubber, the force was impressive.

"Sweet!" Buzz said. "I think this could work."

"Yeah, and no more grubs," Jane said.

"Nice job, Carter," Vanessa told him.

"*Really* nice job," Buzz added.

When Jane looked over, there was something different in Buzz's expression. It was no secret he'd always been jealous of Carter, the jock of the family. But all Jane saw on Buzz's face now was admiration.

And when the two boys traded a fist bump, she knew for sure that something had changed between them. It was as if they'd forgotten they didn't like each other. Maybe that made them friends, and maybe it didn't, but they were definitely turning into brothers out here.

She just wished Mom and Dad were around to see it.

CHAPTER 11

Vanessa's hands shook. It was still early morning, but she'd been up since first light, getting the raft ready to go once and for all. For the last hour or more, that had meant tying dozens of knots to bind the bamboo pieces together as snugly as her strength would allow.

Maybe it was the hunger giving her the shakes. Or maybe it was excitement at the prospect of real food for the family. She'd been inspired by Carter's fishing spear and had barely gotten any sleep thinking about it. If they could just get out on the water, she felt sure they could catch some fish.

Now, with the morning sun shining straight back into the cove, Vanessa made a final check of her work. The raft was finished. It looked like a version of the shelter roof they'd built back at the old beach, just a dozen bamboo poles lashed side by side. It wasn't so much to look at, but the real question was, Would it do the job?

Vanessa's tired muscles drove a little harder as she dragged the raft into the shallow water at the edge of the cove. It floated there, perfectly. That part was no surprise. The bamboo was incredibly buoyant. But it would have to hold their weight, too.

She waded out a little farther and pushed down on the raft with both hands. The bamboo poles clacked against each other and sprang back easily each time.

More importantly, the raft held together as she climbed on board. With a couple of homemade paddles, it was more than enough to get them out to the reef. It would be like having their own movable diving platform.

"Is that our new raft?" Jane's voice came from the direction of the ship.

Vanessa turned to see her standing at the rail.

"Sure is," she said. "Get Buzz and come on down. We're going out fishing!"

———

Carter didn't ask anyone's permission to come along that morning. There was no way he'd be staying back while everyone else did all the work. Not again.

"What about your hand?" Vanessa asked as he climbed onto the raft next to Jane.

"What about it?" Carter said. He picked up one of the two paddles Buzz had made. It was a thick piece of bamboo split down the middle, and the curve of it fit right into the C-shape of his stiff, swollen fingers.

"See? I can even paddle," he said. "It's not like my arms and legs are broken."

"I don't know, Carter," Vanessa said warily.

"You don't have to," he said. "Because I'm not asking."

He expected more of an argument, but Vanessa simply shook her head and set the Hawaiian sling on the raft. Jane took up the second paddle. Buzz had a cloth bag made out of his own shirt, and he tied it to his belt loop with a piece of rope. With any luck, that bag would be heavy with fish by the time they got back. It was time to go.

Carter's head still swam with fever, but he wasn't going to let that stop him. He knew exactly where he wanted to be.

"Let's get going," he said. "The sooner we get out there, the sooner we eat!"

"I hear that," Buzz said, and they pushed off.

The day was calm and windless. Jane and Carter paddled while Vanessa and Buzz stayed in the water, flutter-kicking off the back like a human outboard motor. It all made for easy going as they worked their way past the mouth of the cove and into the open water just off the shore of Nowhere Island.

Looking back, Carter got a view he hadn't had before. The island's cliffs looked even huger from here. It was hard to believe they'd climbed down those rock walls just a few days earlier.

It was also hard to believe that this place was

uncharted, and that nobody had put it on a map by now. But the fact was, there were ten thousand miles of Pacific Ocean all around them. However big the island looked, it was a needle in a watery haystack.

As they paddled farther out, several white blobs with long, thin tentacles passed by the raft on either side. They looked to Carter like half-inflated balloons.

"Jellyfish!" Jane said, pointing down at them.

"Are they edible?" Carter asked, ready to scoop one up with his paddle.

"I don't think so," Jane answered. "In fact, they might be the stinging kind. We should keep moving."

Soon the wide coral reef came into view. The turquoise water here was like wavy glass. Carter could see the colored shapes of fish—*edible* fish—darting in and out of the coral. It looked like a little underwater city. A busy one, too. That was encouraging.

"This is the spot!" Vanessa called out. "Hey, Carter, hand me the sling."

There was no question about who would be going down for the fish. Carter's injured hand and fever meant he was already doing everything he could.

Buzz wasn't much of a diver. And Jane had tried to use the spear, but it was just too big for her.

"Wish me luck," Vanessa said.

"Good luck," Carter said, along with Jane and Buzz at the same time.

Vanessa took three breaths and held the last one. Then she flashed a thumbs-up, flipped over in the water with the spear at her side, and headed down.

CHAPTER 12

As Vanessa made her way down to the reef, it was like escaping from one world into another. Unlike the rest of the island, this place was cool, wet, and amazingly quiet.

A mask and fins would have been a big help, but the water was like crystal. Also, unlike the last time, when they'd dived down to the sunken *Lucky Star*, the reef here was just a short drop from the surface. It took only a few seconds to reach it.

Fish scattered as Vanessa came near but quickly worked their way back in her direction. She saw blurred flashes of color everywhere. A yellow, black, and white fish swam right in front of her. Another, the same blue-green as a tropical parrot, darted between two branches of coral. A school of tiny silver ones flitted by.

This place was like a grocery store, she thought. Time to start shopping.

It wasn't easy, though. It took several trips down, then back up for air, just to get an idea of where the biggest concentration of fish was.

On her fourth dive, Vanessa started figuring out how to stop and float in one position, rather than shooing the fish away with too much movement.

The next time, she started thinking more about the spear. She kept it ready now, held out in front of her with the sling pulled tight.

After each trip down, her technique had improved. On the sixth, seventh, and eighth dives, she managed to get off actual shots at actual fish—but missed every time. Still, the adrenaline of the hunt was enough to keep her going.

On the ninth try, Vanessa swam down to her favorite spot alongside the brown-green wall of coral.

She leveled her body in the water, parallel to the sandy bottom, and floated there, waiting for as long as her lungs would allow.

Out of the coral, a flat, pale-pink-and-white fish the size of her hand nosed forward. It paused to nibble something off the reef, just a few feet away.

Vanessa knew this was the one. She could feel it in her bones before she even fired.

Sling cocked, she released her grip on the shaft and let it fly. It zipped through the water and at nearly the same moment found its mark. The fish shimmied violently back and forth on the tip of the spear, but it had no chance of getting away.

Vanessa let out an underwater scream. "YES!" she cried, sending a stream of bubbles toward the surface. She'd done it. She'd caught her first fish. And this wasn't *just* a fish. This was the beginning of something that could help save their lives.

Keeping a grip on the spear, she turned and kicked her way back toward the raft. She held the fish overhead so it would be the first thing Carter, Jane, and Buzz saw coming out of the water.

But there was no need. Even before she reached the top, she could hear them up there, already screaming for joy.

━━━━━

For a long time, Buzz hung out on the raft with Jane and Carter while Vanessa made one trip down after another. She was like a machine, and it wasn't hard to see why. Every fourth or fifth dive, she managed to come up with something else on her spear. The bag hanging off Buzz's belt loop was so heavy with fish by now, it made his mouth water.

A week ago, they'd been living in a cave, with nothing. Now, they had a dry shelter, a constant source of water, and—finally—an endless supply of food. Was it better than being back home? Not in a million years. But it *was* a million times better than it had been.

As Vanessa surfaced once more, Buzz rolled over to see a little brown and green speckled fish flicking on the sharpened point of her bamboo spear.

"That's five!" she said. "Let's go for one more."

"Up to you," Buzz told her. They already had enough for a meal, but then again, more was more. He lifted the slippery fish off the spear with both hands, being careful not to drop it. Jane held the bag open for him, and he turned to put the fish inside.

As he did, a ripple of movement off to the side caught Buzz's eye.

"I'm going down again," Vanessa said behind him.

"Hold on," Buzz said. The bamboo dug into his knees as he came up higher for a better look.

"What is it?" Jane asked.

"I don't know."

Buzz stared off to the right, his pulse ticking upward. The glinting sun on the water made it hard to see, but *something* was definitely moving toward them. Not a fish. Not a little one, anyway. It was some kind of big, dark shape.

And then, as a triangular gray fin broke the surface, his worst fear was confirmed all at once.

"Vanessa, get up here. *Now!*" he said.

Vanessa didn't question it. She threw the spear

onto the raft and started scrambling on board.

"Carter, wake up!" Jane said, shaking him out of his nap.

"What's going on?" Carter asked.

There was no time to answer. The raft shimmied hard and tilted under Vanessa's weight, throwing Buzz off balance. He reached for an edge, or anything to hold on to, but it was no good. As the others scrabbled toward the middle of the raft, it was already breaking apart underneath them. Jane fell in first. Buzz tried to grab her, but his legs slid between two of the bamboo poles. The gap between them yawned open, and he slipped right through into the ocean. The yell that came out of him quickly turned into a mouthful of seawater. Then a lungful, too.

He choked and coughed under the surface. Sections of bamboo floated free over his head, creating shadows in the water that only confused him more. Twisting around, Buzz tried to spot the oncoming shark, wherever it was. His hand curled into a fist, a pathetic defense against an unbeatable predator.

From behind him, it whizzed by. Buzz flinched hard,

fully expecting the shock of a bite somewhere—his arm, his leg. But no. The thing kept right on moving. All Buzz saw was a receding blue-gray blur.

He popped up to the surface where Jane, Vanessa, and Carter were churning the water as well, all of them struggling to get out of the way. The bag of fish still hung from his belt loop and twisted awkwardly around his legs. He realized it probably made him a floating piece of bait, but he couldn't let the fish go— not even now.

It took some number of endless panic-filled seconds to realize the shark was gone, or at least out of sight. But that didn't stop the five-alarm dose of adrenaline that was still running through Buzz's system.

"Let's get out of here!" he yelled. Everyone grabbed a piece of raft and started kicking toward the shore as fast as they could.

It was only as they were underway that Buzz noticed a sharp stinging pain in his leg. He wasn't sure if it had just happened, or if it had been there all along behind the rush of confusion. But now, it was impossible to ignore. A searing hot tingle ran up from his calf, through his upper leg, and into his entire body.

"You guys, I think I got bit!" he said.

"What?" Vanessa asked. She let go of her own piece of bamboo and swam over to reach Buzz's. "Where'd it get you?"

Buzz reached down and touched the spot on his calf where the pain had started. There was no blood, at least none he could see. But it was hard to tell with all the movement around him. One thing he knew about sharks above all—they could smell tiny amounts of blood over huge distances of water.

"There's nothing we can do out here. Can you make it back?" Vanessa asked.

Buzz only nodded. There was no choice, but the pain and the panic were nearly overwhelming. It was all he could do to kick toward the shore—and pray that he didn't see any signs of a return visit.

As soon as they reached the mouth of the cove, Jane worked with Carter and Vanessa to help Buzz up onto the rocks at the shoreline. His face had gone pale, and his jaw was set in a constant grimace of pain.

Vanessa knelt next to him. "Where does it hurt?" she asked.

"All over," Buzz groaned, and squeezed his eyes shut.

"Where'd you get bit?" Jane asked.

He pointed to his left calf, where an angry red blotch showed on the skin. There were no teeth marks or punctures. Just some kind of raised rash.

"I think that's a jellyfish sting," Jane said. "I'll bet anything."

She pointed at the spot, and Buzz raised his head to see. He nodded in agreement and then lay back again.

"What can we do?" Carter asked.

"I don't know!" Vanessa said.

"You have to . . . pee . . . on it," Buzz gritted out.

"He's right!" Jane said, and looked straight at Carter. "I've heard about this. Peeing on it gets rid of the pain."

"What?" Carter asked. "What do you mean, pee?"

"Like, urinate," Jane said.

"I know what *pee* means, Jane. I'm just asking—"

"JUST DO IT!" Buzz said, with as much force as Jane had ever heard from him.

If anyone was going to do this, it had to be Carter. That went without saying. But Carter wasn't looking so good himself. He'd overdone it—Jane could tell with a glance. He was hunched over with his hands on his knees, as though he were struggling to keep to his feet.

"Okay," he said into the ground. "I've got this."

Without being asked, Jane and Vanessa looked away. Jane squeezed Vanessa's hand and watched the water. It was hard, knowing Buzz was in so much pain, and to hear him groaning there on the rocks.

"Could you hurry up already?" Buzz said behind her.

"I'm working on it," Carter said.

"Just do it. And don't pee on the fish!"

"Just shut up, okay?"

There was a long, silent pause. When Buzz spoke

again, Jane could hear that some of the tension had already left his voice. It sounded as if the peeing had actually worked, and quickly, too.

"By the way, this never happened," Buzz said.

"You're telling me," Carter added, zipping up his shorts.

Jane bit her lip to stop from laughing and kept her eyes on the water. She could see a few loose pieces of bamboo floating out by the reef. One of the paddles was in sight, but the other was gone, along with the Hawaiian sling. They'd have to start all over on a new raft, but at least they still had the fish.

"Hey!" Vanessa shouted out. "It's back!"

Jane turned to look where Vanessa was pointing. A gray fin was just slipping beneath the water's surface. It sent a chill through her, thinking about what could have happened to them out there.

"Buzz, Carter, look!" she said, without turning around. She kept her eyes on the spot where the fin had been a second ago.

And then, a few yards farther off, something big burst out of the water. Jane screamed with surprise.

It came straight up, spun all the way around, and splashed down out of sight.

It hadn't been a shark at all, she realized. It was a dolphin. A spinner dolphin. There had been no real danger to begin with.

Before anyone could respond, another dolphin took to the air. And then another, even farther out. Each one of them landed back in the water and continued on its way as smoothly as any gymnast or acrobat.

There seemed to be a whole family of them. Several more surfaced as the pod went by, showing their dorsal fins and expelling air. Jane couldn't tear her eyes away. She wanted to catch as much of the show as possible. The leapers seemed to spin right out of the water for the sheer pleasure of it. They looked so free, so at home here, each one as beautiful as it was amazing to watch.

"Are you guys seeing this?" she asked.

When Buzz finally answered, it wasn't what she expected to hear. "Carter?" he said. And then, "Carter!"

Now Jane did turn around. Her brother was

swaying on his feet, almost as if he were in a trance.

"I think I, uh . . . need to lie down," he said.

Buzz sat up fast, but Carter was already falling. By the time Jane reached for him, Carter's eyes had rolled back in his head. His knees buckled and he dropped, passed out right there on the rocks.

CHAPTER 13

Carter's mind felt like gray fuzz. The fever kept him in a sweat, while the rest of his body seemed to prickle with goose bumps no matter how close to the fire he stayed.

"I think he's awake," someone said.

"Was I asleep?" Carter asked. He remembered stumbling back to the ship, but not much more. "What time is it?"

"The sun's going down," Vanessa said. "Here, we saved you some fish."

"I'll have some later," he said.

"Don't be stupid," she told him. "You have to eat. It's the only way you'll get stronger."

"I'm not being stupid. I'm just not hungry."

"Are you kidding me?" Vanessa asked. She actually seemed angry. Buzz and Jane were sitting across the fire from him, and they noticed it, too. They both looked over now, with scared, wide-eyed expressions.

When Vanessa spoke again, her voice shook. "In case you hadn't noticed, we're all in this together," she said. "We're a family, Carter. How many times do I have to say that before you get it? Now eat the stupid fish before I kill you."

Carter reached over and pinched off a small amount of the flaky white flesh. When he put it in his mouth, it was warm and comforting. But even so, it was hard for him to swallow. His appetite was gone, and he had no desire to eat more. That was as scary as his swollen hand, which was up to twice the size it had been that morning. A line of dried yellow pus showed along the original wound, and it was impossible to unbend his fingers anymore.

Their long day in the sun, and the swim back, had wrecked him. He'd never felt worse, even on the night he'd spewed his guts out after drinking bad water. The difference this time was, he didn't expect to feel better anytime soon.

"Have some more," Vanessa said. She fed him several mouthfuls of fish. Carter took the food, chewed it, and swallowed—but not because he wanted to.

He did it for the others. Right now, that was the most he could manage.

"Buzz, can you give me a hand down here?" Vanessa asked. "I want to pull together whatever bamboo we have."

"There isn't that much," Buzz said.

"Will you just come here, please?" Vanessa asked, more bossy than usual.

She left the deck and dropped to the ground, leading Buzz around the bow to the water's edge, out of earshot from Jane and Carter. All the salvaged bamboo from the raft sat in a pile on the ground against the hull of the ship.

"What's going on?" Buzz asked. "I thought you wanted to—"

Vanessa raised a finger to her mouth to quiet Buzz. "What do we do about Carter?" she whispered.

Buzz shook his head. "What *can* we do?" he whispered back.

Neither of them seemed to have an answer for that. They stared silently at each other. Finally, Vanessa asked the one thing she'd been trying not to bring up for the last three days. She'd been trying not even to think about it, but there was no avoiding the question.

"Can you die from an infected cut?" she asked. The words caught in her throat, followed quickly by a sob. It felt like bringing the possibility to life, just by naming it.

"I don't know," Buzz answered, clearly fighting back his own tears.

"Nobody ever said anything about infection on those million shows you watched?" Vanessa pressed him. "Come on, Buzz, think. There has to be something we can do."

"I don't know!" he said again, in a fierce whisper. "I wish I did, but . . . I don't."

"Is Carter going to die?"

Vanessa turned to see Jane standing there. She'd always had a way of moving around so as to not be noticed. Now she stood in the shadow of the ship's hull, staring at them as if she were afraid to come any closer.

"I hope not," Vanessa answered. Two weeks ago, she would have tried to hide the truth from Jane. Not anymore.

The sound of cicadas filled Vanessa's ears, while horrible thoughts poured into her mind. Would there be a new grave on the island before it was all over? How would they ever be able to take that if it happened? How could they live without Carter?

She shook her head then, as if to expel the thoughts. Up till now, it had been impossible even to imagine something like that happening. But there was also nothing left to say. Nothing they could do, and very little they could even hope for.

Except maybe a miracle.

CHAPTER 14

The next morning, everyone quietly went about his or her business. Vanessa came outside to find Buzz laying pieces of bamboo side by side for a new raft. He'd already split one piece for a new paddle and had begun sharpening another into a spear.

"How long have you been awake?" she asked.

Buzz shook his head. He hadn't slept, she realized. He'd been up all night, sitting with Carter by the fire and working by torchlight.

It swelled her with a melancholy pride. Her little couch potato of a brother had probably changed more than any of them out here. He certainly wasn't a couch potato anymore. And he wasn't giving up, either.

As sad as she felt, she was also glad to have Buzz here, more than ever.

"I don't think we're going to be able to fish today," he said. "What if you and Jane tried to reach the old camp? We could definitely use some coconut to get us by in the meantime."

Vanessa nodded in agreement. There was so much she wanted to say, but Buzz looked as much on edge as she felt. It seemed best to keep moving and try for the coconut. She put a hand on his shoulder, for just a moment, and then turned to go get Jane.

A few minutes later, she and Jane set out through the woods, following the blazed trail back toward the old camp. They were quiet as they walked, each one busy with her own thoughts. Carter still wasn't eating, and had drunk barely any water that morning. When they left him, he'd been dozing fitfully by the fire. The image of his pale, sweaty face haunted Vanessa in the silence.

Soon, they came to the place where the mudslide had been. Water trickled down the slope, and a long muddy scar cut right through the middle of the woods. It didn't take long to figure out that the mud was still too deep to pass.

"Let's check down by the water," Vanessa said. "Maybe we can get over the rocks now."

They cut left and headed downhill. Keeping to the edge of the gully where the mudslide had torn away most of the vegetation, it was an easy pass straight down to the ocean. It only took a few minutes to reach the water.

Coming out into the open, Vanessa stopped again. The warm sunshine felt good on her face. She took a deep breath and closed her eyes.

"Can we sit for a minute?" she asked. "And maybe imagine we're somewhere else?"

"Where?" Jane asked.

"*Anywhere* else."

Even though there were a million things to do, it felt to Vanessa like more than just a good idea. Right now, it felt necessary. Her mind hadn't stopped running since she'd opened her eyes that morning.

Jane didn't say a word. She sat down on a rock,

pulled her knees up tight, and rested her head there.

Vanessa sat down next to her, cross-legged and facing the ocean. She thought about her room back at home. It was strange to imagine it, just sitting there, exactly the way she'd left it, like some kind of movie on pause.

Did her friends even know what was going on? Were the four Benson-Diaz kids in the news? Did everyone think they were dead by now?

This wasn't helping, Vanessa realized. Maybe it was best just to keep moving.

But then Jane sat up all at once. She looked quizzically at Vanessa.

"What is it?" Vanessa asked.

"Do you hear something?" Jane asked.

"Hear what?"

Jane didn't respond right away. She was zoned in, clearly catching something that Vanessa couldn't. Her head was cocked to the side. Her eyes shifted from left to right as if she were trying to envision the image that went with the sound.

"I think that's an airplane!" she said, and jumped up.

Vanessa leaped up as well. She scanned the horizon but didn't see any sign of a plane. It seemed as if Jane were imagining something she wanted to hear.

"I don't know what you're talking about, Jane," she said. "There's nothing there—"

"Shh!" Jane said. "Just listen."

And then, Vanessa heard it, too. The sound was so small, so faint, they might not have even noticed it if they hadn't stopped for a moment of quiet on this piece of shoreline. But there it was, growing clearer as Vanessa listened.

"Where is it? Do you see anything?" Vanessa asked. The sky still looked as empty as the air had sounded a moment ago. But the faint engine sound was undeniable. It had to be somewhere.

"There!" Jane said. She pointed south and west, down the shore.

Vanessa squinted that way—and sure enough, Jane was right again. There it was. How had she seen something so small? It looked like a tiny insect just floating in the distance. But there was no denying what it was. A plane. *A second chance at a rescue.*

Something she'd begun to think they'd never see.

And maybe this time would be different than the last time.

"We have to light the signal fire!" Jane said, just before they both turned back toward the woods.

Even as Vanessa scrambled uphill, headed for camp, she was screaming Buzz's and Carter's names.

Buzz was sitting with Carter on the deck of the ship when the girls came tearing into the cove.

"Buzz! Get a torch!" Jane yelled. "Now! There's a plane!"

"Hurry!" Vanessa yelled. They were climbing down past the spring and gesturing at him frantically.

Buzz didn't fully understand, but he'd heard the only thing he needed to know. *Plane.* Immediately, he was dipping a new torch into the fire.

Even Carter was up now, looking around. "What do we do?" he said, half slurring.

"We have to light the signal fire!" Buzz said. The

oily rags seemed to take forever, but they finally burst to life. He grasped the flaming torch, jumped off the ship, and ran out toward the mouth of the cove.

"Go grab as much wood as you can!" he yelled at the girls, who had started to follow him. "Anything that'll burn! Bring it out to the fire. I'll get it going!"

Jane and Vanessa turned and headed for the ship. Carter was on his way down, already carrying a few logs under his one good arm.

"I'm not even sure if it's coming this way," Jane called back. "But it's definitely out there."

Buzz could hear the hum of the engine as he came to the place where the cove opened up and gave way to the rocky shoreline of the island. In a flat clearing at the top of the rocks, their signal pyre sat waiting.

"Bring the knife!" he shouted back toward the ship. "We need to cut some fronds!" Fresh green fronds made bright white smoke, he knew. Maybe that would help.

He knelt down and pushed the head of the burning torch into the center of the pyre. The ball of dry grass and kindling there sparked up and started burning right away. That was a good sign, but it had a long way to go if there was any hope of catching the plane's attention.

Buzz looked up along the shore. He could see it now. The plane was far off but definitely headed their way.

"BURN!" he yelled at the fire. It seemed to be taking way too long. He could see Jane and Vanessa carrying one of the old wooden pallets together out toward where he stood. Carter came behind, much more slowly.

Buzz left the fire to burn and raced to the ship. When he reached the deck again, he grabbed the bucket of oil and another load of wood and headed back.

"Do you still see the plane?" he shouted as he ran. The signal fire was burning well now, but it didn't look like enough. His heart clenched at the thought of losing another chance at rescue.

"It's coming!" Jane said. "Hurry, Buzz!"

He reached the others and immediately poured the oil around the base of the flames. The heat of the fire singed his arms, but adrenaline kept him going.

The oil sizzled and smoked for several seconds, then ignited with a burst. It let off a trail of dark smoke, but still, it wasn't enough. The plane was well within sight now. He could see the shape of it. But the real question was—how did they make the plane see *them*?

"We need it bigger!" Buzz yelled. "What else have we got to burn?"

"I'll cut some fronds," Vanessa said. She took the knife and scrambled up toward the woods.

Carter tore off his shirt, wiped it around in the oily bucket, and threw it in. Buzz did the same.

"What else?" Buzz asked. It felt as though the clock on their very last chance was ticking down . . . ticking down. . . .

"I have an idea!" Jane shouted. "Come on, Buzz. Right now!"

She grabbed the torch Buzz had been using and headed back toward the ship. Buzz had no clue what she was thinking, but he took off after her. As he left the signal fire behind, Vanessa was throwing fronds down from the woods, and Carter was doing his best to pile them onto the blaze. Just like everything else, it seemed like too little, too late.

Whatever Jane's idea was, he hoped it was a good one.

CHAPTER 15

Buzz followed Jane up onto the boat, into the wheelhouse, and down through the hatch to the deck below. He hated not being able to see outside anymore, not knowing where the plane was.

"What are you doing?" he called after Jane as they moved up the passage toward the stern.

"We're going to light the oil tank!" Jane said.

It stopped Buzz cold. "What?" he asked. "We can't do that."

"We have to," Jane said. She continued into the small cabin with the manhole cover in the floor. It sat over the opening of the tank, just slightly to the side.

Jane set the burning torch on the metal floor and dropped to her knees. "Help me move this out of the way," she said.

"The whole ship could blow up!" Buzz told her.

"Do you have a better idea?" she asked.

He didn't. Jane was right, and Buzz knew it. In fact, he wondered why he hadn't thought of this himself. Fire was his thing. He'd been thinking about how to make and keep fires for the last thirteen days, nonstop. But Jane's calm focus, despite the urgency of the situation, was infectious.

He knelt down next to her and put his hands on the heavy iron disc. "One, two, three!" he said. They heaved together and twisted the cover off to the side. The smell from down below burned Buzz's nostrils.

Outside, he could hear the sound of the plane. It was getting close.

"Okay," Jane said as she picked up the torch. "Get ready to run like crazy."

"Wait!" Buzz said. He knew what to do. There was no reason for two of them to be down here right now. He reached out and snatched the torch away.

"What are you doing?" Jane said.

"Go," Buzz told her. "I'll light it."

"But—" Jane started to object.

"There's no time, Jane," Buzz cut her off. "Just go. I'll catch up."

"Buzz, you can't!" she said.

He dropped the torch on the floor, put both hands on her shoulders, and shoved her toward the door. "GET OUT!" he screamed. "You're wasting time. Go!"

Jane stumbled into the passage and let out a wail as she ran toward the front.

"Hurry, Buzz!" she called back. "Please hurry!"

Buzz stood in the middle of the cabin and picked up the burning torch. He knew that it usually took a moment before the oil caught fire. With any luck, he'd have just enough time to get out of there. And if not, it could still get the others off this island, once and for all. That was a risk worth taking, especially for Carter's sake. He wouldn't survive much longer.

This was it. One chance to save them. It was crazy—a complete shot in the dark. But Jane was right. They had to try.

He could hear Jane outside now screaming for the others. That was good. It meant she was off the boat.

Buzz checked the door once more to make sure he had a clear way out of the room.

He held the torch over the hole. He positioned his feet like a sprinter ready to fly. Then he took a deep breath and dropped the torch down into the tank.

Vanessa could scarcely believe what Jane was telling her.

"Yes, he's lighting the fuel tank!" she said again. "I'm sorry, it was my idea!"

Vanessa turned toward the ship, running blindly. The plane—headed straight for the island—was forgotten. She had to get Buzz out of there. This was insane.

"Buzz!" she screamed, splashing along the edge of the cove. "Buzz! Don't do it! Get out of there!"

She was halfway back to the boat when she saw Buzz racing through the wheelhouse on his way out.

"Run!" Buzz screamed. He threw himself off the deck and kept going. "Get away, get away, get away!"

Vanessa stopped and reversed direction, with Buzz right behind. The plane was almost directly overhead. If the ship was going to blow it needed to blow now.

"Nothing's happening!" Buzz said, even as they were still moving.

"Are you sure you lit it?" Vanessa said back.

"I don't know, I put the—"

A giant, hollow explosion of sound filled the air. The force of it blew through the cove like a strong wind. Vanessa felt her ears pop. She stumbled just as Buzz caught up to her. They both hit the ground, then turned to look back.

A giant, rolling red-and-orange ball was rising up from the ship. It looked as if the sky itself was on fire. It was huge. The wheelhouse had disintegrated. Vanessa threw an arm over Buzz as debris splashed down in the water and onto the ground around them. A giant piece of railing landed with a crash, just ten feet off to the right.

When she looked up again, Vanessa saw the rolling flames giving way to a black smoke that flowed up and out of the cove, like fumes through a chimney. If anything was going to be seen from a distance, it wasn't their signal fire anymore. It was that explosion.

Adrenaline still pumping, Vanessa grabbed Buzz's hand and ran back to the others.

"YES!" Jane shouted as Buzz and Vanessa raced toward them. It had worked. Somehow, it had worked.

But they weren't through this yet. She stood at the water's edge with Carter, waving and waving at the plane. This was it—the moment when it all came to an end. It had to be. There was no other option, and they all screamed at the sky.

"HELP!"

"DOWN HERE!"

"PLEASE!"

Unbelievably, the airplane never changed its

course. It continued on its way, passing west over the island, while the screaming continued.

"NO! DON'T LEAVE!"

"COME BACK!"

But it was no good. Within a few moments, the plane had disappeared over the tops of the trees. Jane stood with her neck still craned upward, her gaze overhead, where there was nothing left to see anymore.

The plane was gone. Not only that, but the ship was ruined as well. It was all too much—an unbearable load of bad luck. She couldn't hold back her tears.

"I don't understand," she sobbed. "How could they not see us? How could this happen—again?"

"Was it the same plane as the last time?" Vanessa asked.

"I don't know," Jane said. "What does it matter?"

"It doesn't," Vanessa said. "I just . . ." She trailed off, as if she'd realized there was nothing left to say. No way to describe what any of them were feeling. And now she was crying, too. They all were.

It couldn't be true. The plane couldn't have really passed them by. Not *twice*.

And yet, the empty sky over Jane's head told her everything there was to know. The plane had moved on, and the only thing up there now was a huge black cloud of smoke, as the ship behind them—their home—burned up in flames.

Just like their chances of being rescued.

Carter didn't even try to wipe away his tears. The pain in his hand was nothing compared to the torture of watching another rescue slip right through their fingers.

And there had been nothing he could do to help. All he'd managed was a few weak shouts at the sky, watching the speck of a plane fly over, with a horrible sense of déjà vu.

He lay back on the rocks now, feeling empty. Not just in his stomach, but in his heart, too. Everywhere. Everything. The emptiness consumed him. It felt . . . over.

Nobody said a word for a long time. They all sank

to the ground around him, catching their breath at first, then crying quietly to themselves. There was simply nothing to say.

In fact, if there had been any conversation, Carter might not have heard the soft hum of the plane, coming closer again.

But he did hear it. At first, he stayed silent, thinking it might just be his imagination playing tricks on him. It wasn't until he saw Buzz look up, and then both of the girls, too, that he let himself believe it might be true.

"Is that . . . ?" Buzz said.

"Really?" Jane said, turning around in a full circle, scanning the sky again.

There was no mistaking it now. The plane had looped around from the west and was headed back in their direction.

"They must have seen the smoke!" Vanessa said. "That has to be it!"

"They're coming back! They're coming back!" Jane sang out.

And then sure enough, over the tops of the trees, the beautiful sight of an airplane appeared. It was flying lower than before—much lower. This was a plane getting ready to land. But where? There wasn't enough room on the island.

Carter could see now that this wasn't the same craft from the other day. It was red and white, with big pontoons underneath. This was a seaplane—it could land on water.

He waved, while his brother and sisters jumped up and down, screaming as loudly as they could.

It was an unbelievable sight. An unbelievable feeling, too. Like some kind of dream he'd had more than once since they'd landed on Nowhere Island. And now it was coming true.

The plane flew in a wide arc, out over the ocean to the east, and then back again, heading straight at them. The others held Carter up on his feet as it skimmed down onto the water, propellers buzzing, less than fifty yards offshore.

It was hard for Carter to make out what Vanessa and Buzz were even saying, there was so much excitement in their voices. Jane was crying too hard for words.

He could see the pilot behind the seaplane's small windshield. There were others on board as well, moving around inside as they continued to float closer. Soon, the door on the side opened.

And even now, with everything that had just happened, the last person Carter expected to see was the first off the plane.

"MOMMY!" Jane screamed, finding her voice.

Beth Benson reached toward them, still twenty yards away, her face crumpled up with tears of her own. Behind her, Eric Diaz emerged onto the pontoon.

"Dad!" Buzz and Vanessa yelled simultaneously.

Behind their parents, two of the flight crew had already launched a bright yellow dinghy. One of them was handing red-and-white boxes of what Carter guessed to be medical supplies down to the other.

But Mom wasn't waiting. She plunged into the water followed by Dad, and they started swimming for the beach.

It was too much for Carter. It was as if his mind didn't know how to process what was happening. All the fears—that they might never be rescued, that his infection might kill him—were gone. The feeling went way beyond words. There were only tears now.

Tears of joy.

Vanessa, Jane, and Buzz raced into the water toward their parents. Carter was moving, too, more slowly. Before they'd gotten very far, Buzz stopped and turned around to come back. He put an arm around Carter to hold him up, and they continued on together.

"We did it, Carter," Buzz said. "I don't know how—but we did."

Before Carter could say anything, they were both swallowed up in their parents' arms. Jane and Vanessa were there, too—a six-person huddle of tears and screams, with everyone talking at once.

"It's a miracle!" Dad said.

"How'd you find us?" Vanessa asked.

"You're here, you're here! You're really here!" Jane cheered.

"Look at you!" Mom said. "I can't believe this!"

"We're okay," Buzz was saying. "I think we're okay."

Only Carter stayed silent. His legs wobbled

underneath him, while the others held him up. His hand throbbed as badly as ever, and the fever put a soft blur on everything he saw and heard around him. He wasn't out of the woods yet. He knew that.

But he'd never felt so safe in his life as he did right now.

CHAPTER 16

July 11. LAST DAY ON NOWHERE ISLAND

You know what's better than snails??? Peanut M&M's. And bottled water. And turkey sandwiches. And granola bars.

And having my mom and dad right here in front of my eyes. And hugging them, and knowing I never have to stop if I don't want to.

And my mom's voice telling me everything is going to be okay again.

And knowing that we're going home.

I'm going to write that again. WE'RE GOING HOME.

Mom told me that Joe and Uncle Dex are safe and sound. They had to go to the hospital for a little while, but they're going to be just fine. She also said that she and Dad have been flying their own hired plane all over the place for days—even double-checking the sections that the Coast Guard had already checked. And guess what? It worked, because here they are.

Carter's in the worst shape, by far. I'm watching them give him intravenous medicine and taking good care of him, right here on the island. The floatplane is too small for all of us, so the pilots are going to fly back and get a helicopter to come pick us up! I've never been in a helicopter!

Good-bye, snails. Good-bye, mud and rain and mosquitoes, and grubs and snakes and ants, and wild boars and everything else about this place. I won't ever forget you, Nowhere Island, but I can't wait to start trying.

Already, Mom and Dad have a million questions. Mostly they want to know how we did this.

Dad said, "You guys are a real miracle. How did you survive?"

And I liked Buzz's answer.

He said, "Together."

READ HOW THE ADVENTURE BEGAN IN

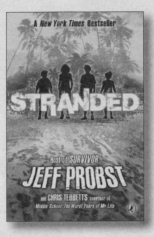

A family vacation becomes a test of survival.

It was supposed to be a vacation—and a chance to get to know one another better. But when a massive storm sets in without warning, four kids are ship-wrecked alone on a rocky jungle island in the middle of the South Pacific. No adults. No instructions. Nobody to rely upon but themselves. Can they make it home alive?

A week ago, the biggest challenge Vanessa, Buzz, Carter, and Jane had was learning to live as a new blended family. Now the four siblings must find a way to work together if they're going to make it off the island. But first they've got to learn to survive one another.

CHAPTER 1

It was day four at sea, and as far as eleven-year-old Carter Benson was concerned, life didn't get any better than this.

From where he hung, suspended fifty feet over the deck of the *Lucky Star*, all he could see was a planet's worth of blue water. The boat's huge white mainsail ballooned in front of him, filled with a stiff southerly wind that sent them scudding through the South Pacific faster than they'd sailed all week.

This was the best part of the best thing Carter had ever done, no question. It was like sailing and flying at the same time. The harness around his middle held him in place while his arms and legs hung free. The air itself seemed to carry him along, at speed with the boat.

"How you doin' up there, Carter?" Uncle Dexter shouted from the cockpit.

Carter flashed a thumbs-up and pumped his fist. "Faster!" he shouted back. Even with the wind whipping in his ears, Dex's huge belly laugh came back, loud and clear.

Meanwhile, Carter had a job to do. He wound the safety line from his harness in a figure eight around the cleat on the mast to secure himself. Then he reached over and unscrewed the navigation lamp he'd come up here to replace.

As soon as he'd pocketed the old lamp in his rain slicker, he pulled out the new one and fitted it into the fixture, making sure not to let go before he'd tightened it down. Carter had changed plenty of lightbulbs before, but never like this. If anything, it was all too easy and over too fast.

When he was done, he unwound his safety line and gave a hand signal to Dex's first mate, Joe

Kahali, down below. Joe put both hands on the winch at the base of the mast and started cranking Carter back down to the deck.

"Good job, Carter," Joe said, slapping him on the back as he got there. Carter swelled with pride and adrenaline. Normally, replacing the bulb would have been Joe's job, but Dex trusted him to take care of it.

Now Joe jerked a thumb over his shoulder. "Your uncle wants to talk to you," he said.

Carter stepped out of the harness and stowed it in its locker, just like Dex and Joe had trained him to do. Once that was done, he clipped the D-ring on his life jacket to the safety cable that ran the length of the deck and headed toward the back.

It wasn't easy to keep his footing as the *Lucky Star* pitched and rolled over the waves, but even that was part of the fun. If he did fall, the safety cable—also called a jackline—would keep him from going overboard. Everyone was required to stay clipped in when they were on deck, whether they were up there to work . . . or to puke, like Buzz was doing right now.

"Gross! Watch out, Buzz!" Carter said, pushing past him.

"*Uhhhhhnnnnh,*" was all Buzz said in return. He was leaning against the rail and looked both green and gray at the same time.

Carter kind of felt sorry for him. They were both eleven years old, but they didn't really have anything else in common. It was like they were having two different vacations out here.

"Gotta keep moving," he said, and continued on toward the back, where Dex was waiting.

"Hey, buddy, it's getting a little choppier than I'd like," Dex said as Carter stepped down into the cockpit. "I need you guys to get below."

"I don't want to go below," Carter said. "Dex, I can help. Let me steer!"

"No way," Dex said. "Not in this wind. You've been great, Carter, but I promised your mom before we set sail—no kids on deck if these swells got over six feet. You see that?" He pointed to the front of the boat, where a cloud of sea spray had just broken over the bow. "*That's* what a six-foot swell looks like. We've got a storm on the way—maybe a big one. It's time for you to take a break."

"Come on, please?" Carter said. "I thought we came out here to sail!"

Dex took him by the shoulders and looked him square in the eye.

"Remember what we talked about before we set out? My boat. My rules. Got it?"

Carter got it, all right. Arguing with Dex was like wrestling a bear. You could try, but you were never going to win.

"Now, grab your brother and get down there," Dex told him.

"Okay, fine," Carter said. "But he's not my brother, by the way. Just because my mom married his dad doesn't mean—"

"Ask me tomorrow if I care," Dexter said, and gave him a friendly but insistent shove. "Now go!"

Benjamin "Buzz" Diaz lifted his head from the rail

and looked out into the distance. All he could see from here was an endless stretch of gray clouds over an endless stretch of choppy waves.

Keeping an eye on the horizon was supposed to help with the seasickness, but so far, all it had done was remind him that he was in the middle of the biggest stretch of nowhere he'd ever seen. His stomach felt like it had been turned upside down and inside out. His legs were like rubber bands, and his head swam with a thick, fuzzy feeling, while the boat rocked and rocked and rocked.

It didn't look like this weather was going to be changing anytime soon, either. At least, not for the better.

Buzz tried to think about something else—anything else—to take his mind off how miserable he felt. He thought about his room back home. He thought about how much he couldn't wait to get there, where he could just close his door and hang out all day if he wanted, playing City of Doom and eating pepperoni pizz—

Wait, Buzz thought. *No. Not that.*

He tried to unthink anything to do with food, but it was too late. Already, he was leaning over the rail again and hurling the last of his breakfast into the ocean.

"Still feeding the fish, huh?" Suddenly, Carter was back. He put a hand on Buzz's arm. "Come on," he said. "Dex told me we have to get below."

Buzz clutched his belly. "Are you kidding?" he said. "Can't it wait?"

"No. Come on."

All week long, Carter had been running around the deck of the *Lucky Star* like he owned it or something. Still, Carter was the least of Buzz's worries right now.

It was only day four at sea, and if things kept going like this, he was going to be lucky to make it to day five.

Vanessa Diaz sat at the *Lucky Star*'s navigation station belowdecks and stared at the laptop screen in front of her. She'd only just started to learn about this stuff a few days earlier, but as far as she could tell, all that orange and red on the weather radar was a bad sign. Not to mention the scroll across the bottom of the screen, saying something about "gale-force winds and deteriorating conditions."

The first three days of their trip had been nothing but clear blue skies and warm breezes. Now, nine hundred miles off the coast of Hawaii, all of that had changed. Dexter kept saying they had to adjust their course to outrun the weather, but so far, it seemed like the weather was outrunning them. They'd changed direction at least three times, and things only seemed to be getting worse.

The question was—how *much* worse?

A chill ran down Vanessa's spine as the hatch over the galley stairs opened, and Buzz and Carter came clattering down the steps.

"How are you feeling, Buzzy?" she asked, but he didn't stop to talk. Instead, he went straight for the little bathroom—the "head," Dexter called it—and slammed the door behind him.

Her little brother was getting the worst of these bad seas, by far. Carter, on the other hand, seemed unfazed.

Sometimes Vanessa called them "the twins," as a joke, because they were both eleven but nothing alike. Carter kept his sandy hair cut short and was even kind of muscley for a kid his age. Buzz, on the other hand, had shaggy jet-black curls like their father's and was what adults liked to call husky. The kids at school just called him fat.

Vanessa didn't think her brother was fat—not exactly—but you could definitely tell he spent a lot of time in front of the TV.

"It's starting to rain," Carter said, looking up at the sky.

"Then close the hatch," Vanessa said.

"Don't tell me what to do."

Vanessa rolled her eyes. "Okay, fine. Get wet. See if I care."

He would, too, she thought. He'd just stand there and get rained on, only because she told him not to. Carter was one part bulldog and one part mule.

Jane was there now, too. She'd just come out of the tiny sleeping cabin the two girls shared.

Jane was like the opposite of Carter. She could slip in and out of a room without anyone ever noticing. With Carter, you always knew he was there.

"What are you looking at, Nessa?" Jane asked.

"Nothing." Vanessa flipped the laptop closed. "I was just checking the weather," she said.

There was no reason to scare Jane about all that. She was only nine, and tiny for her age. Vanessa was the oldest, at thirteen, and even though nobody told her to look out for Jane on this trip, she did anyway.

"Dex said there's a storm coming," Carter blurted out. "He said it's going to be major."

"Carter!" Vanessa looked over at him and rolled her eyes in Jane's direction.

But he just shrugged. "What?" he said. "You think she's not going to find out?"

"You don't have to worry about me," Jane said.

She crawled up onto Vanessa's lap and opened the computer to have a look. "Show me."

"See?" Carter said. "I know my sister."

Vanessa took a deep breath. If the idea of this trip was to make them one big happy family, it wasn't exactly working.

Technically, the whole sailing adventure was a wedding gift from her new uncle, Dexter. It had been two months since Vanessa and Buzz's father had married Carter and Jane's mother, but they'd waited until the end of the school year to take a honeymoon. Now, while their parents were hiking Volcanoes National Park and enjoying the beaches on Hawaii's Big Island, the four kids were spending the week at sea and supposedly getting to know one another better.

So far, the sailing had been amazing, but the sister-brother bonding thing? Not so much, Vanessa thought. The weather wasn't helping, either. It looked like they were going to be cooped up together for the rest of the day.

"Is that the storm?" Jane said. She pointed at the large red mass on the laptop screen.

"That's it," Vanessa answered. On the computer, it seemed as if the oncoming front had gotten even bigger in the last few minutes. She started braiding Jane's long blond hair to distract her.

"It's just rain, right?" Jane said. "If this was something really bad, we'd already know about it. Wouldn't we, Nessa?"

Vanessa tried to smile. "Sure," she said. But the truth was, she had no idea how bad it was going to get.

None of them did.

GET MORE OF THE ADVENTURE IN

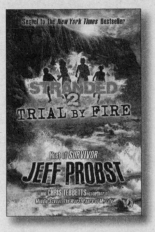

They thought it couldn't get any worse. They were wrong.

Being shipwrecked on a jungle island in the middle of the South Pacific was bad enough. But now that Carter, Vanessa, Buzz, and Jane have lost their boat—and almost everything on board—to another violent storm, it's like starting over. That means finding food and shelter, making fire for the first time, dealing with the wild boars that roam the island—and of course, figuring out how to get along (and not kill each other in the process). Survival is no individual sport in a place like this, but there's only one way to learn that. The hard way.

JEFF PROBST (www.jeffprobst.com) is the multi-Emmy Award—winning host and executive producer of the popular series *Survivor*. He is also the founder of the Serpentine Project, a nonprofit organization designed to help young adults transition out of the foster care system, and has worked with the larger nonprofit organization Alliance for Children's Rights, which has provided one hundred thousand kids in Los Angeles with free legal assistance and advocacy. Each season, *Survivor* memorabilia is auctioned off, and to date, the auctions have raised hundreds of thousands of dollars for the organization.

A native of Wichita, Kansas, Probst is married and lives in Los Angeles with his wife and two children when not traveling the world.

He can be followed on Twitter @jeffprobst and online at www.jeffprobst.com.

CHRIS TEBBETTS is the *New York Times* bestselling coauthor of James Patterson's Middle School series. Originally from Yellow Springs, Ohio, Tebbetts is a graduate of Northwestern University. He lives and writes in Vermont.